From This World to the Next by Henry Fielding

Henry Fielding was born at Sharpham in Somerset on April 22nd, 1707.

His most famous and well loved work is 'Tom Jones'. A classic.

Fielding's history is certainly colourful and rich in texture. A novelist and playwright, he was not averse to causing controversy or even scandal but he was also a magistrate and helped to establish the Police force.

He was educated at Eton College, where he established a lifelong friendship with William Pitt the Elder. After a few romantic problems he journeyed to London to establish a literary career. By 1728 he was off to Leiden to study classics and law at the University.

Funds did not last too long and he was forced to return to London and to begin writing for the theatre. Much of his work was witheringly critical of Sir Robert Walpole's government. His satires were always on the edge and the Establishment was not amused. The Theatrical Licensing Act of 1737 seems to have Fielding's activities as one of its targets. Once the Act passed, political satire on the stage was almost impossible. Fielding retired from the theatre and resumed his career in law and, in order to support his wife Charlotte Craddock, whom he had married in 1734, and children, he became a barrister. Charlotte was the basis for the heroines of both 'Tom Jones' and 'Amelia'.

His lack of financial sense meant that he and his family often endured periods of poverty, but he was helped by Ralph Allen, a wealthy benefactor who later formed the basis of Squire Allworthy in Tom Jones.

In 1742 Fielding published 'Joseph Andrews' one of his major works.

When Charlotte died in 1744 they had produced five children but only one, Henrietta, survived (and she only until age 23).

Three years after Charlotte's death, disregarding public opinion, he married her former maid, Mary Daniel, who was also pregnant. Society was not impressed but it certainly was in character. Mary bore five children, three daughters who died young and sons William and Allen.

Politics at the time were certainly unusual but conspired to help. Despite the scandal, his consistent anti-Jacobitism and support for the Church of England it led to him being rewarded a year later with the position of London's Chief Magistrate, and his literary career went from strength to strength.

Joined by his younger half-brother John, he helped found what some have called London's first police force, the Bow Street Runners, in 1749.

That same year he published what was to be his literary masterpiece 'Tom Jones' together with 'From This World To The Next'. It was quite a year.

According to the historian G. M. Trevelyan, the Fielding's "were two of the best magistrates in eighteenth-century London, and did a great deal to enhance the cause of judicial reform and improve prison conditions". His influential pamphlets and enquiries included a proposal for the abolition of public hangings, though he seemed to have less reservation if these were in private.

Fielding started a fortnightly periodical titled The Covent-Garden Journal, which he would publish under the pseudonym of "Sir Alexander Drawcansir, Knt. Censor of Great Britain" until November of the same year. In this periodical, Fielding directly challenged the "armies of Grub Street" and the contemporary periodical writers of the day in a conflict that would eventually become the Paper War of 1752–3.

He then published "Examples of the interposition of Providence in the Detection and Punishment of Murder (1752), a treatise in which, rejecting the deistic and materialistic visions of the world, he wrote in favor of the belief in God's presence and divine judgement,] arguing that the rise of murder rates was due to neglect of the Christian religion. In 1753 he would write Proposals for making an effectual Provision for the Poor.

Fielding's commitment to the cause of justice as a great humanitarian in the 1750s coincided with a rapid deterioration in his health. This continued to such an extent that he went abroad to Portugal in 1754 in search of a cure for his gout, asthma and other afflictions.

Henry fielding died in Lisbon two months later on October 8th, 1754. He is buried in the city's English Cemetery (Cemitério Inglês), which is now the graveyard of St. George's Church, Lisbon.

Index Of Contents

INTRODUCTION

Whether the ensuing pages were really the dream or vision of some very pious and holy person; or whether they were really written in the other world, and sent back to this, which is the opinion of many (though I think too much inclining to superstition); or lastly, whether, as infinitely the greatest part imagine, they were really the production of some choice inhabitant of New Bethlehem, is not necessary nor easy to determine. It will be abundantly sufficient if I give the reader an account by what means they came into my possession. Mr. Robert Powney, stationer, who dwells opposite to Catherine-street in the Strand, a very honest man and of great gravity of countenance; who, among other excellent stationery commodities, is particularly eminent for his pens, which I am abundantly bound to acknowledge, as I owe to their peculiar goodness that my manuscripts have by any means been legible: this gentleman, I say, furnished me some time since with a bundle of those pens, wrapped up with great care and caution, in a very large sheet of paper full of characters, written as it seemed in a very bad hand. Now, I have a surprising curiosity to read everything which is almost illegible; partly perhaps from the sweet remembrance of the dear Scrawls, Skrawls, or Skrales (for the word is variously spelled), which I have in my youth received from that lovely part of the creation for which I have the tenderest regard; and partly from that temper of mind which makes men set an immense value on old manuscripts so effaced, bustoes so maimed, and pictures so black that no one can tell what to make of them. I therefore perused this sheet with wonderful application, and in about a day's time discovered that I could not understand it. I immediately repaired to Mr. Powney, and inquired very eagerly whether he had not more of the same manuscript? He produced about one hundred pages, acquainting me that he had saved no more; but that the book was originally a huge folio, had been left in his garret by a gentleman who lodged there, and who had left him no other satisfaction for nine months' lodging. He proceeded to inform me that the manuscript had been hawked about (as he phrased it) among all the booksellers, who refused to meddle; some alleged that they could not read, others that they could not understand it. Some would haze it to be an atheistical book, and some that it was a libel on the government; for one or other of which reasons they all refused to print it. That it had been likewise shown to the R--l Society, but they shook their heads, saying, there was nothing in it wonderful enough for them. That, hearing the gentleman was gone to the West-Indies, and believing it to be good for nothing else, he had used it as waste paper. He said I was welcome to what remained, and he was heartily sorry for what was missing, as I seemed to set some value on it.

I desired him much to name a price: but he would receive no consideration farther than the payment of a small bill I owed him, which at that time he said he looked on as so much money given him.

I presently communicated this manuscript to my friend parson Abraham Adams, who, after a long and careful perusal, returned it me with his opinion that there was more in it than at first appeared; that the author seemed not entirely unacquainted with the writings of Plato; but he wished he had quoted him sometimes in his margin, that I might be sure (said he) he had read him in the original:

for nothing, continued the parson, is commoner than for men now-a-days to pretend to have read Greek authors, who have met with them only in translations, and cannot conjugate a verb in mi.

To deliver my own sentiments on the occasion, I think the author discovers a philosophical turn of thinking, with some little knowledge of the world, and no very inadequate value of it. There are some indeed who, from the vivacity of their temper and the happiness of their station, are willing to consider its blessings as more substantial, and the whole to be a scene of more consequence than it is here represented: but, without controverting their opinions at present, the number of wise and good men who have thought with our author are sufficient to keep him in countenance: nor can this be attended with any ill inference, since he everywhere teaches this moral: That the greatest and truest happiness which this world affords, is to be found only in the possession of goodness and virtue; a doctrine which, as it is undoubtedly true, so hath it so noble and practical a tendency, that it can never be too often or too strongly inculcated on the minds of men.

BOOK I

CHAPTER I

The author dies, meets with Mercury, and is by him conducted to the stage which sets out for the other world.

On the first day of December 1741 [1] I departed this life at my lodgings in Cheapside. My body had been some time dead before I was at liberty to quit it, lest it should by any accident return to life: this is an injunction imposed on all souls by the eternal law of fate, to prevent the inconveniences which would follow. As soon as the destined period was expired (being no longer than till the body is become perfectly cold and stiff) I began to move; but found myself under a difficulty of making my escape, for the mouth or door was shut, so that it was impossible for me to go out at it; and the windows, vulgarly called the eyes, were so closely pulled down by the fingers of a nurse, that I could by no means open them. At last I perceived a beam of light glimmering at the top of the house (for such I may call the body I had been inclosed in), whither ascending, I gently let myself down through a kind of chimney, and issued out at the nostrils.

No prisoner discharged from a long confinement ever tasted the sweets of liberty with a more exquisite relish than I enjoyed in this delivery from a dungeon wherein I had been detained upwards of forty years, and with much the same kind of regard I cast my eyes [2] backwards upon it.

My friends and relations had all quitted the room, being all (as I plainly overheard) very loudly quarreling below stairs about my will; there was only an old woman left above to guard the body, as I apprehend. She was in a fast sleep, occasioned, as from her savor it seemed, by a comfortable dose of gin. I had no pleasure in this company, and, therefore, as the window was wide open, I sallied forth into the open air: but, to my great astonishment, found myself unable to fly, which I had always during my habitation in the body conceived of spirits; however, I came so lightly to the ground that I did not hurt myself; and, though I had not the gift of flying (owing probably to my having neither feathers nor wings), I was capable of hopping such a prodigious way at once, that it served my turn almost as well. I had not hopped far before I perceived a tall young gentleman in a silk waistcoat, with a wing on his left heel, a garland on his head, and a caduceus in his right hand. [3] I thought I had seen this person before, but had not time to recollect where, when he called out to me and asked me how long I had been departed. I answered I was just come forth. "You must not stay here," replied he, "unless you had been murdered: in which case, indeed, you might have been suffered to walk some time; but if you died a natural death you must set out for the other world immediately." I desired to know the way. "O," cried the gentleman, "I will show you to the inn whence the stage proceeds; for I am the porter. Perhaps you never heard of me, my name is Mercury." "Sure, sir," said I, "I have seen you at the play-house." Upon which he smiled, and, without satisfying me as to that point, walked directly forward, bidding me hop after him. I obeyed him, and soon found myself in Warwick-lane; where Mercury, making a full stop, pointed at a particular house, where he bade me enquire for the stage, and, wishing me a good journey, took his leave, saying he must go seek after other customers.

I arrived just as the coach was setting out, and found I had no reason for inquiry; for every person seemed to know my business the moment I appeared at the door: the coachman told me his horses were to, but that he had no place left; however, though there were already six, the passengers offered to make room for me. I thanked them, and ascended without much ceremony. We immediately began our journey, being seven in number; for, as the women wore no hoops, three of them were but equal to two men. Perhaps, reader, thou mayest be pleased with an account of this whole equipage, as peradventure thou wilt not, while alive, see any such. The coach was made by an eminent toyman, who is well known to deal in immaterial substance, that being the matter of which it was compounded. The work was so extremely fine, that it was entirely invisible to the human eye. The horses which drew this extraordinary vehicle were all spiritual, as well as the passengers. They had, indeed, all died in the service of a certain postmaster; and as for the coachman, who was a very thin piece of immaterial substance, he had the honor while alive of driving the Great Peter, or Peter the Great, in whose service his soul, as well as body, was almost starved to death. Such was the vehicle in which I set out, and now, those who are not willing to travel on with me may, if they please, stop here; those who are, must proceed to the subsequent chapters, in which this journey is continued.

CHAPTER II

In which the author first refutes some idle opinions concerning spirits, and then the passengers relate their several deaths.

It is the common opinion that spirits, like owls, can see in the dark; nay, and can then most easily be perceived by others. For which reason, many persons of good understanding, to prevent being terrified with such objects, usually keep a candle burning by them, that the light may prevent their seeing. Mr. Locke, in direct opposition to this, hath not doubted to assert that you may see a spirit in open daylight full as well as in the darkest night.

It was very dark when we set out from the inn, nor could we see any more than if every soul of us had been alive. We had traveled a good way before any one offered to open his mouth; indeed, most of the company were fast asleep, [4] but, as I could not close my own eyes, and perceived the spirit who sat opposite to me to be likewise awake, I began to make overtures of conversation, by complaining HOW DARK IT WAS. "And extremely cold too," answered my fellow traveler; "though, I thank God, as I have no body, I feel no inconvenience from it: but you will believe, sir, that this frosty air must seem very sharp to one just issued forth out of an oven; for such was the inflamed habitation I am lately departed from." "How did you come to your end, sir?" said I. "I was murdered, sir," answered the gentleman. "I am surprised then," replied I, "that you did not divert yourself by walking up and down and playing some merry tricks with the murderer." "Oh, sir," returned he, "I had not that privilege, I was lawfully put to death. In short, a physician set me on fire, by giving me medicines to throw out my distemper. I died of a hot regimen, as they call it, in the small-pox."

One of the spirits at that word started up and cried out, "The small-pox! bless me! I hope I am not in company with that distemper, which I have all my life with such caution avoided, and have so happily escaped hitherto!" This fright set all the passengers who were awake into a loud laughter; and the gentleman, recollecting himself, with some confusion, and not without blushing, asked pardon, crying, "I protest I dreamed that I was alive." "Perhaps, sir," said I, "you died of that distemper, which therefore made so strong an impression on you." "No, sir," answered he, "I never had it in my life; but the continual and dreadful apprehension it kept me so long under cannot, I see, be so immediately eradicated. You must know, sir, I avoided coming to London for thirty years together, for fear of the small-pox, till the most urgent business brought me thither about five days ago. I was so dreadfully afraid of this disease that I refused the second night of my arrival to sup with a friend whose wife had recovered of it several months before, and the same evening got a surfeit by eating too many muscles, which brought me into this good company."

"I will lay a wager," cried the spirit who sat next him, "there is not one in the coach able to guess my distemper." I desired the favor of him to acquaint us with it, if it was so uncommon. "Why, sir," said he, "I died of honor." - "Of honor, sir!" repeated I, with some surprise. "Yes, sir," answered the spirit, "of honor, for I was killed in a duel."

"For my part," said a fair spirit, "I was inoculated last summer, and had the good fortune to escape with a very few marks on my face. I esteemed myself now perfectly happy, as I imagined I had no restraint to a full enjoyment of the diversions of the town; but within a few days after my coming up I caught cold by overdancing myself at a ball, and last night died of a violent fever."

After a short silence which now ensued, the fair spirit who spoke last, it being now daylight, addressed herself to a female who sat next her, and asked her to what chance they owed the happiness of her company. She answered, she apprehended to a consumption, but the physicians were not agreed concerning her distemper, for she left two of them in a very hot dispute about it when she came out of her body. "And pray, madam," said the same spirit to the sixth passenger, "How came you to leave the other world?" But that female spirit, screwing up her mouth, answered, she wondered at the curiosity of some people; that perhaps persons had already heard some reports of her death, which were far from being true; that, whatever was the occasion of it, she was glad at being delivered from a world in which she had no pleasure, and where there was nothing but nonsense and impertinence; particularly among her own sex, whose loose conduct she had long been entirely ashamed of.

The beauteous spirit, perceiving her question gave offense, pursued it no farther. She had indeed all the sweetness and good-humor which are so extremely amiable (when found) in that sex which tenderness most exquisitely becomes. Her countenance displayed all the cheerfulness, the good-nature, and the modesty, which diffuse such brightness round the beauty of Seraphina, [5] awing every beholder with respect, and, at the same time, ravishing him with admiration. Had it not been indeed for our conversation on the small-pox, I should have imagined we had been honored with her identical presence. This opinion might have been heightened by the good sense she uttered whenever she spoke, by the delicacy of her sentiments, and the complacence of her behavior, together with a certain dignity which attended every look, word, and gesture; qualities which could not fail making an impression on a heart [6] so capable of receiving it as mine, nor was she long in raising in me a very violent degree of seraphic love. I do not intend by this, that sort of love which men are very properly said to make to women in the lower world, and which seldom lasts any longer than while it is making. I mean by seraphic love an extreme delicacy and tenderness of friendship, of which, my worthy reader, if thou hast no conception, as it is probable thou mayest not, my endeavor to instruct thee would be as fruitless as it would be to explain the most difficult problems of Sir Isaac Newton to one ignorant of vulgar arithmetic.

To return therefore to matters comprehensible by all understandings: the discourse now turned on the vanity, folly, and misery of the lower world, from which every passenger in the coach expressed the highest satisfaction in being delivered; though it was very remarkable that, notwithstanding the joy we declared at our death, there was not one of us who did not mention the accident which occasioned it as a thing we would have avoided if we could. Nay, the very grave lady herself, who was the forwardest in testifying her delight, confessed inadvertently that she left a physician by her bedside; and the gentleman who died of honor very liberally cursed both his folly and his fencing. While we were entertaining ourselves with these matters, on a sudden a most offensive smell began to invade our nostrils. This very much resembled the savor which travelers in summer perceive at their approach to that beautiful village of the Hague, arising from those delicious canals which, as they consist of standing water, do at that time emit odors greatly agreeable to a Dutch taste, but not so pleasant to any other. Those perfumes, with the assistance of a fair wind, begin to affect persons of quick olfactory nerves at a league's distance, and increase gradually as you approach. In the same manner did the smell I have just mentioned, more and more invade us, till one of the spirits, looking out of the coach-window, declared we were just arrived at a very large city; and indeed he had scarce said so before we found ourselves in the suburbs, and, at the same time, the coachman, being asked by another, informed us that the name of this place was the City of Diseases. The road to it was extremely smooth, and, excepting the above-mentioned savor, delightfully pleasant. The streets of the suburbs were lined with bagnios, taverns, and cooks' shops: in the first we saw several beautiful women, but in tawdry dresses, looking out at the windows; and in the latter were visibly exposed all kinds of the richest dainties; but on our entering the city we found, contrary to all we had seen in the other world, that the suburbs were infinitely pleasanter than the city itself. It was indeed a very dull, dark, and melancholy place. Few people appeared in the streets, and these, for the most part, were old women, and here and there a formal grave gentleman, who seemed to be thinking, with large tie-wigs on, and amber-headed canes in their hands. We were all in hopes that our vehicle would not stop here; but, to our sorrow, the coach soon drove into an inn, and we were obliged to alight.

CHAPTER III

The adventures we met with in the City of Diseases.

We had not been long arrived in our inn, where it seems we were to spend the remainder of the day, before our host acquainted us that it was customary for all spirits, in their passage through that city, to pay their respects to that lady Disease, to whose assistance they had owed their deliverance from the lower world. We answered we should not fail in any complacence which was usual to others; upon which our host replied he would immediately send porters to conduct us. He had not long quitted the room before we were attended by some of those grave persons whom I have before described in large tie-wigs with amber-headed canes. These gentlemen are the ticket-porters in the city, and their canes are the insignia, or tickets, denoting their office. We informed them of the several ladies to whom we were obliged, and were preparing to follow them, when on a sudden they all stared at one another, and left us in a hurry, with a frown on every countenance. We were surprised at this behavior, and presently summoned the host, who was no sooner acquainted with it than he burst into an hearty laugh, and told us the reason was, because we did not fee the gentlemen the moment they came in, according to the custom of the place. We answered, with some confusion, we had brought nothing with us from the other world, which we had been all our lives informed was not lawful to do. "No, no, master," replied the host; "I am apprised of that, and indeed it was my fault. I should have first sent you to my lord Scrape, [7] who would have supplied you with what you want." "My lord Scrape supply us!" said I, with astonishment: "sure you must know we cannot give him security; and I am convinced he never lent a shilling without it in his life." "No, sir," answered the host, "and for that reason he is obliged to do it here, where he is sentenced to keep a bank, and to distribute money gratis to all passengers. This bank originally consisted of just that sum, which he had miserably hoarded up in the other world, and he is to perceive it decrease visibly one shilling a-day, till it is totally exhausted; after which he is to return to the other world, and perform the part of a miser for seventy years; then, being purified in the body of a hog, he is to enter the human species again, and take a second trial." "Sir," said I, "you tell me wonders: but if his bank be to decrease only a shilling a day, how can he furnish all passengers?" "The rest," answered the host, "is supplied again; but in a manner which I cannot easily explain to you." "I apprehend," said I, "this distribution of his money is inflicted on him as a punishment; but I do not see how it can answer that end, when he knows it is to be restored to him again. Would it not serve the purpose as well if he parted only with the single shilling, which it seems is all he is really to lose?" "Sir," cries the host, "when you observe the agonies with which he parts with every guinea, you will be of another opinion. No prisoner condemned to death ever begged so heartily for transportation as he, when he received his sentence, did to go to hell, provided he might carry his money with him. But you will know more of these things when you arrive at the upper world; and now, if you please, I will attend you to my lord's, who is obliged to supply you with whatever you desire."

We found his lordship sitting at the upper end of a table, on which was an immense sum of money, disposed in several heaps, every one of which would have purchased the honor of some patriots and the chastity of some prudes. The moment he saw us he turned pale, and sighed, as well apprehending our business. Mine host accosted him with a familiar air, which at first surprised me, who so well remembered the respect I had formerly seen paid this lord by men infinitely superior in quality to the person who now saluted him in the following manner: "Here, you lord, and be damned to your little sneaking soul, tell out your money, and supply your betters with what they want. Be quick, sirrah, or I'll fetch the beadle to you. Don't fancy yourself in the lower world again, with your privilege at your a--." He then shook a cane at his lordship, who immediately began to tell out his money, with the same miserable air and face which the miser on our stage wears while he delivers his bank-bills. This affected some of us so much that we had certainly returned with no more than what would have been sufficient to fee the porters, had not our host, perceiving our compassion, begged us not to spare a fellow who, in the midst of immense wealth, had always refused the least contribution to charity. Our hearts were hardened with this reflection, and we all filled our pockets with his money. I remarked a poetical spirit, in particular, who swore he would have a hearty gripe at him: "For," says he, "the rascal not only refused to subscribe to my works, but sent back my letter unanswered, though I am a better gentleman than himself." We now returned from this miserable object, greatly admiring the propriety as well as justice of his punishment, which consisted, as our host informed us, merely in the delivering forth his money; and, he observed, we could not wonder at the pain this gave him, since it was as reasonable that the bare parting with money should make him miserable as that the bare having money without using it should have made him happy. Other tie-wig porters (for those we had summoned before refused to visit us again) now attended us; and we having fee'd them the instant they entered the room, according to the instructions of our host, they bowed and smiled, and offered to introduce us to whatever disease we pleased.

We set out several ways, as we were all to pay our respects to different ladies. I directed my porter to show me to the Fever on the Spirits, being the disease which had delivered me from the flesh. My guide and I traversed many streets, and knocked at several doors, but to no purpose. At one, we were told, lived the Consumption; at another, the Maladie Alamode, a French lady; at the third, the

Dropsy; at the fourth, the Rheumatism; at the fifth, Intemperance; at the sixth, Misfortune. I was tired, and had exhausted my patience, and almost my purse; for I gave my porter a new fee at every blunder he made: when my guide, with a solemn countenance, told me he could do no more; and marched off without any farther ceremony.

He was no sooner gone than I met another gentleman with a ticket, i. e., an amber-headed cane in his hand. I first fee'd him, and then acquainted him with the name of the disease. He cast himself for two or three minutes into a thoughtful posture, then pulled a piece of paper out of his pocket, on which he wrote something in one of the Oriental languages, I believe, for I could not read a syllable: he bade me carry it to such a particular shop, and, telling me it would do my business, he took his leave.

Secure, as I now thought myself, of my direction, I went to the shop, which very much resembled an apothecary's. The person who officiated, having read the paper, took down about twenty different jars, and, pouring something out of every one of them, made a mixture, which he delivered to me in a bottle, having first tied a paper round the neck of it, on which were written three or four words, the last containing eleven syllables. I mentioned the name of the disease I wanted to find out, but received no other answer than that he had done as he was ordered, and the drugs were excellent. I began now to be enraged, and, quitting the shop with some anger in my countenance, I intended to find out my inn, but, meeting in the way a porter whose countenance had in it something more pleasing than ordinary, I resolved to try once more, and clapped a fee into his hand. As soon as I mentioned the disease to him he laughed heartily, and told me I had been imposed on, for in reality no such disease was to be found in that city. He then inquired into the particulars of my case, and was no sooner acquainted with them than he informed me that the Maladie Alamode was the lady to whom I was obliged. I thanked him, and immediately went to pay my respects to her. The house, or rather palace, of this lady was one of the most beautiful and magnificent in the city. The avenue to it was planted with sycamore trees, with beds of flowers on each side; it was extremely pleasant but short. I was conducted through a magnificent hall, adorned with several statues and bustoes, most of them maimed, whence I concluded them all to be true antiques; but was informed they were the figures of several modern heroes, who had died martyrs to her ladyship's cause. I next mounted through a large painted staircase, where several persons were depicted in caricatura; and, upon inquiry, was told they were the portraits of those who had distinguished themselves against the lady in the lower world. I suppose I should have known the faces of many physicians and surgeons, had they not been so violently distorted by the painter. Indeed, he had exerted so much malice in his work, that I believe he had himself received some particular favors from the lady of this mansion: it is difficult to conceive a group of stranger figures. I then entered a long room, hung round with the pictures of women of such exact shapes and features that I should have thought myself in a gallery of beauties, had not a certain sallow paleness in their complexions given me a more distasteful idea. Through this I proceeded to a second apartment, adorned, if I may so call it, with the figures of old ladies. Upon my seeming to admire at this furniture, the servant told me with a smile that these had been very good friends of his lady, and had done her eminent service in the lower world. I immediately recollected the faces of one or two of my acquaintance, who had formerly kept bagnios; but was very much surprised to see the resemblance of a lady of great distinction in such company. The servant, upon my mentioning this, made no other answer than that his lady had pictures of all degrees. I was now introduced into the presence of the lady herself. She was a thin, or rather meager, person, very wan in the countenance, had no nose and many pimples in her face. She offered to rise at my entrance, but could not stand. After many compliments, much congratulation on her side, and the most fervent expressions of gratitude on mine, she asked me many questions concerning the situation of her affairs in the lower world; most of which I answered to her entire satisfaction. At last, with a kind of forced smile, she said, "I suppose the pill and drop go on swimmingly?" I told her they were reported to have done great cures. She replied she could apprehend no danger from any person who was not of regular practice; "for, however simple mankind are," said she, "or however afraid they are of death, they prefer dying in a regular manner to being cured by a nostrum." She then expressed great pleasure at the account I gave her of the beau monde. She said she had herself removed the hundreds of Drury to the hundreds of Charing-cross, and was very much delighted to find they had spread into St. James's; that she imputed this chiefly to several of her dear and worthy friends, who had lately published their excellent works, endeavoring to extirpate all notions of religion and virtue; and particularly to the deserving author of the Bachelor's Estimate; "to whom," said she, "if I had not reason to think he was a surgeon, and had therefore written from mercenary views, I could never sufficiently own my obligations." She spoke likewise greatly in approbation of the method, so generally used by parents, of marrying children very young, and without the least affection between the parties; and concluded by saying that, if these fashions continued to spread, she doubted not but she should shortly be the only disease who would ever receive a visit from any person of considerable rank.

While we were discoursing her three daughters entered the room. They were all called by hard names; the eldest was named Lepra, the second Chaeras, and the third Scorbutia. [8] They were all genteel, but ugly. I could not help observing the little respect they paid their parent, which the old lady remarking in my countenance, as soon as they quitted the room, which soon happened, acquainted me with her unhappiness in her offspring, every one of which had the confidence to deny themselves to be her children, though she said she had been a very indulgent mother and had plentifully provided for them all. As family complaints generally as much tire the hearer as they relieve him who makes them, when I found her launching farther into this subject I resolved to put an end to my visit, and, taking my leave with many thanks for the favor she had done me, I returned to the inn, where I found my fellow-travelers just mounting into their vehicle. I shook hands with my host and accompanied them into the coach, which immediately after proceeded on its journey.

CHAPTER IV

Discourses on the road, and a description of the palace of Death.

We were all silent for some minutes, till, being well shaken into our several seats, I opened my mouth first, and related what had happened to me after our separation in the city we had just left.

The rest of the company, except the grave female spirit whom our reader may remember to have refused giving an account of the distemper which occasioned her dissolution, did the same. It might be tedious to relate these at large; we shall therefore only mention a very remarkable inveteracy which the Surfeit declared to all the other diseases, especially to the Fever, who, she said, by the roguery of the porters, received acknowledgments from numberless passengers which were due to herself. "Indeed," says she, "those cane-headed fellows" (for so she called them, alluding, I suppose, to their ticket) "are constantly making such mistakes; there is no gratitude in those fellows; for I am sure they have greater obligations to me than to any other disease, except the Vapors." These relations were no sooner over than one of the company informed us we were approaching to the most noble building he had ever beheld, and which we learned from our coachman was the palace of Death. Its outside, indeed, appeared extremely magnificent. Its structure was of the Gothic order; vast beyond imagination, the whole pile consisting of black marble. Rows of immense yews form an amphitheater round it of such height and thickness that no ray of the sun ever perforates this grove, where black eternal darkness would reign was it not excluded by innumerable lamps which are placed in pyramids round the grove; so that the distant reflection they cast on the palace, which is plentifully gilt with gold on the outside, is inconceivably solemn. To this I may add the hollow murmur of winds constantly heard from the grove, and the very remote sound of roaring waters. Indeed, every circumstance seems to conspire to fill the mind with horror and consternation as we approach to this palace, which we had scarce time to admire before our vehicle stopped at the gate, and we were desired to alight in order to pay our respects to his most mortal majesty (this being the title which it seems he assumes). The outward court was full of soldiers, and, indeed, the whole very much resembled the state of an earthly monarch, only more magnificent. We passed through several courts into a vast hall, which led to a spacious staircase, at the bottom of which stood two pages, with very grave countenances, whom I recollected afterwards to have formerly been very eminent undertakers, and were in reality the only dismal faces I saw here; for this palace, so awful and tremendous without, is all gay and sprightly within; so that we soon lost all those dismal and gloomy ideas we had contracted in approaching it. Indeed, the still silence maintained among the guards and attendants resembled rather the stately pomp of eastern courts; but there was on every face such symptoms of content and happiness that diffused an air of cheerfulness all round. We ascended the staircase and passed through many noble apartments whose walls were adorned with various battle-pieces in tapistry, and which we spent some time in observing. These brought to my mind those beautiful ones I had in my lifetime seen at Blenheim, nor could I prevent my curiosity from inquiring where the Duke of Marlborough's victories were placed (for I think they were almost the only battles of any eminence I had read of which I did not meet with); when the skeleton of a beef-eater, shaking his head, told me a certain gentleman, one Lewis XIV, who had great interest with his most mortal majesty, had prevented any such from being hung up there. "Besides," says he, "his majesty hath no great respect for that duke, for he never sent him a subject he could keep from him, nor did he ever get a single subject by his means but he lost 1000 others for him." We found the presence-chamber at our entrance very full, and a buzz ran through it, as in all assemblies, before the principal figure enters; for his majesty was not yet come out. At the bottom of the room were two persons in close conference, one with a square black cap on his head, and the other with a robe embroidered with flames of fire. These, I was informed, were a judge long since dead, and an inquisitor-general. I overheard them disputing with great eagerness whether the one had hanged or the other burned the most. While I was listening to this dispute, which seemed to be in no likelihood of a speedy decision, the emperor entered the room and placed himself between two figures, one of which was remarkable for the roughness, and the other for the beauty of his appearance. These were, it seems, Charles XII of Sweden and Alexander of Macedon. I was at too great a distance to hear any of the conversation, so could only satisfy my curiosity by contemplating the several personages present, of whose names I informed myself by a page, who looked as pale and meager as any court-page in the other world, but was somewhat more modest. He showed me here two or three Turkish emperors, to whom his most mortal majesty seemed to express much civility. Here were likewise several of the Roman emperors, among whom none seemed so much caressed as Caligula, on account, as the page told me, of his pious wish that he could send all the Romans hither at one blow. The reader may be perhaps surprised that I saw no physicians here; as indeed I was myself, till informed that they were all departed to the city of Diseases, where they were busy in an experiment to purge away the immortality of the soul.

It would be tedious to recollect the many individuals I saw here, but I cannot omit a fat figure, well dressed in the French fashion, who was received with extraordinary complacence by the emperor, and whom I imagined to be Lewis XIV himself; but the page acquainted me he was a celebrated French cook. We were at length introduced to the royal presence, and had the honor to kiss hands. His majesty asked us a few questions, not very material to relate, and soon after retired. When we returned into the yard we found our caravan ready to set out, at which we all declared ourselves well pleased; for we were sufficiently tired with the formality of a court, notwithstanding its outward splendor and magnificence.

CHAPTER V

The travelers proceed on their journey, and meet several spirits who are coming into the flesh.

We now came to the banks of the great river Cocytus, where we quitted our vehicle, and passed the water in a boat, after which we were obliged to travel on foot the rest of our journey; and now we met, for the first time, several passengers traveling to the world we had left, who informed us they were souls going into the flesh.

The two first we met were walking arm-in-arm, in very close and friendly conference; they informed us that one of them was intended for a duke, and the other for a hackney-coachman. As we had not yet arrived at the place where we were to deposit our passions, we were all surprised at the familiarity which subsisted between persons of such different degrees; nor could the grave lady help expressing her astonishment at it. The future coachman then replied, with a laugh, that they had exchanged lots; for that the duke had with his dukedom drawn a shrew for a wife, and the coachman only a single state.

As we proceeded on our journey we met a solemn spirit walking alone with great gravity in his countenance: our curiosity invited us, notwithstanding his reserve, to ask what lot he had drawn.

He answered, with a smile, he was to have the reputation of a wise man with L100,000 in his pocket, and was practicing the solemnity which he was to act in the other world. A little farther we met a company of very merry spirits, whom we imagined by their mirth to have drawn some mighty lot, but, on inquiry, they informed us they were to be beggars.

The farther we advanced, the greater numbers we met; and now we discovered two large roads leading different ways, and of very different appearance; the one all craggy with rocks, full as it seemed of boggy grounds, and everywhere beset with briars, so that it was impossible to pass through it without the utmost danger and difficulty; the other, the most delightful imaginable, leading through the most verdant meadows, painted and perfumed with all kinds of beautiful flowers; in short, the most wanton imagination could imagine nothing more lovely. Notwithstanding which, we were surprised to see great numbers crowding into the former, and only one or two solitary spirits choosing the latter.

On inquiry, we were acquainted that the bad road was the way to greatness, and the other to goodness. When we expressed our surprise at the preference given to the former we were acquainted that it was chosen for the sake of the music of drums and trumpets, and the perpetual acclamations of the mob, with which those who traveled this way were constantly saluted. We were told likewise that there were several noble palaces to be seen, and lodged in, on this road, by those who had passed through the difficulties of it (which indeed many were not able to surmount), and great quantities of all sorts of treasure to be found in it; whereas the other had little inviting more than the beauty of the way, scarce a handsome building, save one greatly resembling a certain house by the Bath, to be seen during that whole journey; and, lastly, that it was thought very scandalous and mean-spirited to travel through this, and as highly honorable and noble to pass by the other. We now heard a violent noise, when, casting our eyes forwards, we perceived a vast number of spirits advancing in pursuit of one whom they mocked and insulted with all kinds of scorn. I cannot give my reader a more adequate idea of this scene than by comparing it to an English mob conducting a pickpocket to the water; or by supposing that an incensed audience at a playhouse had unhappily possessed themselves of the miserable damned poet. Some laughed, some hissed, some squalled, some groaned, some bawled, some spit at him, some threw dirt at him. It was impossible not to ask who or what the wretched spirit was whom they treated in this barbarous manner; when, to our great surprise, we were informed that it was a king: we were likewise told that this manner of behavior was usual among the spirits to those who drew the lots of emperors, kings, and other great men, not from envy or anger, but mere derision and contempt of earthly grandeur; that nothing was more common than for those who had drawn these great prizes (as to us they seemed) to exchange them with tailors and cobblers; and that Alexander the Great and Diogenes had formerly done so; he that was afterwards Diogenes having originally fallen on the lot of Alexander. And now, on a sudden, the mockery ceased, and the king-spirit, having obtained a hearing, began to speak as follows; for we were now near enough to hear him distinctly:

"Gentlemen, I am justly surprised at your treating me in this manner, since whatever lot I have drawn, I did not choose: if, therefore, it be worthy of derision, you should compassionate me, for it might have fallen to any of your shares. I know in how low a light the station to which fate hath assigned me is considered here, and that, when ambition doth not support it, it becomes generally so intolerable, that there is scarce any other condition for which it is not gladly exchanged: for what portion, in the world to which we are going, is so miserable as that of care? Should I therefore consider myself as become by this lot essentially your superior, and of a higher order of being than the rest of my fellow-creatures; should I foolishly imagine myself without wisdom superior to the wise, without knowledge to the learned, without courage to the brave, and without goodness and virtue to the good and virtuous; surely so preposterous, so absurd a pride, would justly render me the object of ridicule. But far be it from me to entertain it. And yet, gentlemen, I prize the lot I have drawn, nor would I exchange it with any of yours, seeing it is in my eye so much greater than the rest. Ambition, which I own myself possessed of, teaches me this; ambition, which makes me covet praise, assures me that I shall enjoy a much larger proportion of it than can fall within your power either to deserve or obtain. I am then superior to you all, when I am able to do more good, and when I execute that power. What the father is to the son, the guardian to the orphan, or the patron to his client, that am I to you. You are my children, to whom I will be a father, a guardian, and a patron. Not one evening in my long reign (for so it is to be) will I repose myself to rest without the glorious, the heart-warming consideration, that thousands that night owe their sweetest rest to me. What a delicious fortune is it to him whose strongest appetite is doing good, to have every day the opportunity and the power of satisfying it! If such a man hath ambition, how happy is it for him to be seated so on high, that every act blazes abroad, and attracts to him praises tainted with neither sarcasm nor adulation, but such as the nicest and most delicate mind may relish! Thus, therefore, while you derive your good from me, I am your superior. If to my strict distribution of justice you owe the safety of your property from domestic enemies; if by my vigilance and valor you are protected from foreign foes; if by my encouragement of genuine industry, every science, every art which can embellish or sweeten life, is produced and flourishes among you; will any of you be so insensible or ungrateful as to deny praise and respect to him by whose care and conduct you enjoy these blessings? I wonder not at the censure which so frequently falls on those in my station; but I wonder that those in my station so frequently deserve it. What strange perverseness of nature! What wanton delight in mischief must taint his composition, who prefers dangers, difficulty, and disgrace, by doing evil, to safety, ease, and honor, by doing good! who refuses happiness in the other world, and heaven in this, for misery there and hell here! But, be assured, my intentions are different. I shall always endeavor the ease, the happiness, and the glory of my people, being confident that, by so doing, I take the most certain method of procuring them all to myself." He then struck directly into the road of goodness, and received such a shout of applause as I never remember to have heard equaled. He was gone a little way when a spirit limped after him, swearing he would fetch him back.

This spirit, I was presently informed, was one who had drawn the lot of his prime minister.

CHAPTER VI

An account of the wheel of fortune, with a method of preparing a spirit for this world.

We now proceeded on our journey, without staying to see whether he fulfilled his word or no; and without encountering anything worth mentioning, came to the place where the spirits on their passage to the other world were obliged to decide by lot the station in which every one was to act there. Here was a monstrous wheel, infinitely larger than those in which I had formerly seen lottery-tickets deposited. This was called the WHEEL OF FORTUNE.

The goddess herself was present. She was one of the most deformed females I ever beheld; nor could I help observing the frowns she expressed when any beautiful spirit of her own sex passed by her, nor the affability which smiled in her countenance on the approach of any handsome male spirits. Hence I accounted for the truth of an observation I had often made on earth, that nothing is more fortunate than handsome men, nor more unfortunate than handsome women. The reader may be perhaps pleased with an account of the whole method of equipping a spirit for his entrance into the flesh.

First, then, he receives from a very sage person, whose look much resembled that of an apothecary (his warehouse likewise bearing an affinity to an apothecary's shop), a small phial inscribed, THE PATHETIC POTION, to be taken just before you are born. This potion is a mixture of all the passions, but in no exact proportion, so that sometimes one predominates, and sometimes another; nay, often in the hurry of making up, one particular ingredient is, as we were informed, left out. The spirit receiveth at the same time another medicine called the NOUSPHORIC DECOCTION, of which he is to drink ad libitum. This decoction is an extract from the faculties of the mind, sometimes extremely strong and spirituous, and sometimes altogether as weak; for very little care is taken in the preparation. This decoction is so extremely bitter and unpleasant, that, notwithstanding its wholesomeness, several spirits will not be persuaded to swallow a drop of it, but throw it away, or give it to any other who will receive it; by which means some who were not disgusted by the nauseousness drank double and treble portions. I observed a beautiful young female, who, tasting it immediately from curiosity, screwed up her face and cast it from her with great disdain, whence advancing presently to the wheel, she drew a coronet, which she clapped up so eagerly that I could not distinguish the degree; and indeed I observed several of the same sex, after a very small sip, throw the bottles away. As soon as the spirit is dismissed by the operator, or apothecary, he is at liberty to approach the wheel, where he hath a right to extract a single lot: but those whom Fortune favors she permits sometimes secretly to draw three or four. I observed a comical kind of figure who drew forth a handful, which, when he opened, were a bishop, a general, a privy-counselor, a player, and a poet-laureate, and, returning the three first, he walked off, smiling, with the two last. Every single lot contained two more articles, which were generally disposed so as to render the lots as equal as possible to each other; on one was written, EARL, RICHES, HEALTH, DISQUIETUDE; on another, COBLER, SICKNESS, GOOD-HUMOR; on a third, POET, CONTEMPT, SELF-SATISFACTION; on a fourth, GENERAL, HONOR, DISCONTENT; on a fifth, COTTAGE, HAPPY LOVE; on a sixth, COACH AND SIX, IMPOTENT JEALOUS HUSBAND; on a seventh, PRIME MINISTER, DISGRACE; on an eighth, PATRIOT, GLORY; on a ninth, PHILOSOPHER, POVERTY, EASE; on a tenth, MERCHANT, RICHES, CARE. And indeed the whole seemed to contain such a mixture of good and evil, that it would have puzzled me which to choose. I must not omit here that in every lot was directed whether the drawer should marry or remain in celibacy, the married lots being all marked with a large pair of horns. We were obliged, before we quitted this place, to take each of us an emetic from the apothecary, which immediately purged us of all our earthly passions, and presently the cloud forsook our eyes, as it doth those of Aeneas in Virgil, when removed by Venus; and we discerned things in a much clearer light than before. We began to compassionate those spirits who were making their entry into the flesh, whom we had till then secretly envied, and to long eagerly for those delightful plains which now opened themselves to our eyes, and to which we now hastened with the utmost eagerness. On our way we met with several spirits with very dejected countenances; but our expedition would not suffer us to ask any questions. At length we arrived at the gate of Elysium. Here was a prodigious crowd of spirits waiting for admittance, some of whom were admitted, and some were rejected; for all were strictly examined by the porter, whom I soon discovered to be the celebrated judge Minos.

CHAPTER VII

The proceedings of Judge Minos at the gate of Elysium.

I now got near enough to the gate to hear the several claims of those who endeavored to pass. The first among other pretensions, set forth that he had been very liberal to an hospital; but Minos answered, "Ostentation," and repulsed him. The second exhibited that he had constantly frequented his church, been a rigid observer of fast-days: he likewise represented the great animosity he had shown to vice in others, which never escaped his severest censure; and as to his own behavior, he had never been once guilty of whoring, drinking, gluttony, or any other excess. He said he had disinherited his son for getting a bastard. "Have you so?" said Minos; "then pray return into the other world and beget another; for such an unnatural rascal shall never pass this gate." A dozen others, who had advanced with very confident countenances, seeing him rejected, turned about of their own accord, declaring, if he could not pass, they had no expectation, and accordingly they followed him back to earth; which was the fate of all who were repulsed, they being obliged to take a further purification, unless those who were guilty of some very heinous crimes, who were hustled in at a little back gate, whence they tumbled immediately into the bottomless pit.

The next spirit that came up declared he had done neither good nor evil in the world; for that since his arrival at man's estate he had spent his whole time in search of curiosities; and particularly in the study of butterflies, of which he had collected an immense number. Minos made him no answer, but with great scorn pushed him back. There now advanced a very beautiful spirit indeed. She began to ogle Minos the moment she saw him. She said she hoped there was some merit in refusing a great number of lovers, and dying a maid, though she had had the choice of a hundred. Minos told her she had not refused enow yet, and turned her back.

She was succeeded by a spirit who told the judge he believed his works would speak for him. "What works?" answered Minos. "My dramatic works," replied the other, "which have done so much good in recommending virtue and punishing vice." "Very well," said the judge; "if you please to stand by, the first person who passes the gate by your means shall carry you in with him; but, if you will take my advice, I think, for expedition sake, you had better return, and live another life upon earth." The bard grumbled at this, and replied that, besides his poetical works, he had done some other good things: for that he had once lent the whole profits of a benefit-night to a friend, and by that means had saved him and his family from destruction. Upon this the gate flew open, and Minos desired him to walk in, telling him, if he had mentioned this at first, he might have spared the remembrance of his plays. The poet answered, he believed, if Minos had read his works, he would set a higher value on them. He was then beginning to repeat, but Minos pushed him forward, and, turning his back to him, applied himself to the next passenger, a very genteel spirit, who made a very low bow to Minos, and then threw himself into an erect attitude, and imitated the motion of taking snuff with his right hand. Minos asked him what he had to say for himself. He answered, he would dance a minuet with any spirit in Elysium: that he could likewise perform all his other exercises very well, and hoped he had in his life deserved the character of a perfect fine gentleman. Minos replied it would be great pity to rob the world of so fine a gentleman, and therefore desired him to take the other trip. The beau bowed, thanked the judge, and said he desired no better.

Several spirits expressed much astonishment at this his satisfaction; but we were afterwards informed he had not taken the emetic above mentioned.

A miserable old spirit now crawled forwards, whose face I thought I had formerly seen near Westminster Abbey. He entertained Minos with a long harangue of what he had done when in the HOUSE; and then proceeded to inform him how much he was worth, without attempting to produce a single instance of any one good action. Minos stopped the career of his discourse, and acquainted him he must take a trip back again.

"What! to S---- house?" said the spirit in an ecstasy; but the judge, without making him any answer, turned to another, who with a very solemn air and great dignity, acquainted him he was a duke. "To the right-about, Mr. Duke," cried Minos, "you are infinitely too great a man for Elysium;" and then, giving him a kick on the b--ch, he addressed himself to a spirit who, with fear and trembling, begged he might not go to the bottomless pit: he said he hoped Minos would consider that, though he had gone astray, he had suffered for it, that it was necessity which drove him to the robbery of eighteenpence, which he had committed, and for which he was hanged, that he had done some good actions in his life, that he had supported an aged parent with his labor, that he had been a very tender husband and a kind father, and that he had ruined himself by being bail for his friend. At which words the gate opened, and Minos bade him enter, giving him a slap on the back as he passed by him. A great number of spirits now came forwards, who all declared they had the same claim, and that the captain should speak for them. He acquainted the judge that they had been all slain in the service of their country. Minos was going to admit them, but had the curiosity to ask who had been the invader, in order, as he said, to prepare the back gate for him. The captain answered they had been the invaders themselves, that they had entered the enemy's country, and burned and plundered several cities. "And for what reason?" said Minos. "By the command of him who paid us," said the captain; "that is the reason of a soldier. We are to execute whatever we are commanded, or we should be a disgrace to the army, and very little deserve our pay." "You are brave fellows indeed," said Minos; "but be pleased to face about, and obey my command for once, in returning back to the other world: for what should such fellows as you do where there are no cities to be burned, nor people to be destroyed? But let me advise you to have a stricter regard to truth for the future, and not call the depopulating other countries the service of your own." The captain answered, in a rage, "Damn me! do you give me the lie?" and was going to take Minos by the nose had not his guards prevented him, and immediately turned him and all his followers back the same road they came.

Four spirits informed the judge that they had been starved to death through poverty, being the father, mother, and two children; that they had been honest and as industrious as possible, till sickness had prevented the man from labor. "All that is very true," cried a grave spirit who stood by. "I know the fact; for these poor people were under my cure." "You was, I suppose, the parson of the parish," cries Minos; "I hope you had a good living, sir." "That was but a small one," replied the spirit; "but I had another a little better." - "Very well," said Minos; "let the poor people pass." At which the parson was stepping forwards with a stately gait before them; but Minos caught hold of him and pulled him back, saying, "Not so fast, doctor, you must take one step more into the other world first; for no man enters that gate without charity." A very stately figure now presented himself, and, informing Minos he was a patriot, began a very florid harangue on public virtue and the liberties of his country. Upon which Minos showed him the utmost respect, and ordered the gate to be opened.

The patriot was not contented with this applause; he said he had behaved as well in place as he had done in the opposition; and that, though he was now obliged to embrace the court measures, yet he had behaved very honestly to his friends, and brought as many in as was possible. "Hold a moment," says Minos: "on second consideration, Mr. Patriot, I think a man of your great virtue and abilities will be so much missed by your country, that, if I might advise you, you should take a journey back again. I am sure you will not decline it; for I am certain you will, with great readiness, sacrifice your own happiness to the public good." The patriot smiled, and told Minos he believed he was in jest; and was offering to enter the gate, but the judge laid fast hold of him and insisted on his return, which the patriot still declining, he at last ordered his guards to seize him and conduct him back.

A spirit now advanced, and the gate was immediately thrown open to him before he had spoken a word. I heard some whisper, "That is our last lord mayor."

It now came to our company's turn. The fair spirit which I mentioned with so much applause in the beginning of my journey passed through very easily; but the grave lady was rejected on her first appearance, Minos declaring there was not a single prude in Elysium.

The judge then addressed himself to me, who little expected to pass this fiery trial. I confessed I had indulged myself very freely with wine and women in my youth, but had never done an injury to any man living, nor avoided an opportunity of doing good; that I pretended to very little virtue more than general philanthropy and private friendship. I was proceeding, when Minos bade me enter the gate, and not indulge myself with trumpeting forth my virtues. I accordingly passed forward with my lovely companion, and, embracing her with vast eagerness, but spiritual innocence, she returned my embrace in the same manner, and we both congratulated ourselves on our arrival in this happy region, whose beauty no painting of the imagination can describe.

CHAPTER VIII

The adventures which the author met on his first entrance into Elysium.

We pursued our way through a delicious grove of orange-trees, where I saw infinite numbers of spirits, every one of whom I knew, and was known by them (for spirits here know one another by intuition). I presently met a little daughter whom I had lost several years before. Good gods! what words can describe the raptures, the melting passionate tenderness, with which we kissed each other, continuing in our embrace, with the most ecstatic joy, a space which, if time had been measured here as on earth, could not be less than half a year.

The first spirit with whom I entered into discourse was the famous Leonidas of Sparta. I acquainted him with the honors which had been done him by a celebrated poet of our nation; to which he answered he was very much obliged to him. We were presently afterwards entertained with the most delicious voice I had ever heard, accompanied by a violin, equal to Signior Piantinida. I presently discovered the musician and songster to be Orpheus and Sappho.

Old Homer was present at this concert (if I may so call it), and Madam Dacier sat in his lap. He asked much after Mr. Pope, and said he was very desirous of seeing him; for that he had read his Iliad in his translation with almost as much delight as he believed he had given others in the original. I had the curiosity to inquire whether he had really writ that poem in detached pieces, and sung it about as ballads all over Greece, according to the report which went of him. He smiled at my question, and asked me whether there appeared any connection in the poem; for if there did he thought I might answer myself. I then importuned him to acquaint me in which of the cities which contended for the honor of his birth he was really born? To which he answered, "Upon my soul I can't tell."

Virgil then came up to me, with Mr. Addison under his arm. "Well, sir," said he, "how many translations have these few last years produced of my Aeneid?" I told him I believed several, but I could not possibly remember; for that I had never read any but Dr. Trapp's. "Ay," said he, "that is a curious piece indeed!" I then acquainted him with the discovery made by Mr. Warburton of the Elusinian mysteries couched in his sixth book. "What mysteries?" said Mr. Addison. "The Elusinian," answered Virgil, "which I have disclosed in my sixth book." "How!" replied Addison. "You never mentioned a word of any such mysteries to me in all our acquaintance." "I thought it was unnecessary," cried the other, "to a man of your infinite learning: besides, you always told me you perfectly understood my meaning." Upon this I thought the critic looked a little out of countenance, and turned aside to a very merry spirit, one Dick Steele, who embraced him, and told him he had been the greatest man upon earth; that he readily resigned up all the merit of his own works to him. Upon which Addison gave him a gracious smile, and, clapping him on the back with much solemnity, cried out, "Well said, Dick!"

I then observed Shakespeare standing between Betterton and Booth, and deciding a difference between those two great actors concerning the placing an accent in one of his lines: this was disputed on both sides with a warmth which surprised me in Elysium, till I discovered by intuition that every soul retained its principal characteristic, being, indeed, its very essence. The line was that celebrated one in Othello -

PUT OUT THE LIGHT, AND THEN PUT OUT THE LIGHT according to Betterton. Mr. Booth contended to have it thus:

Put out the light, and then put out THE light. I could not help offering my conjecture on this occasion, and suggested it might perhaps be -

Put out the light, and then put out THY light. Another hinted a reading very sophisticated in my opinion -

Put out the light, and then put out THEE, light, making light to be the vocative case. Another would have altered the last word, and read -

PUT OUT THY LIGHT, AND THEN PUT OUT THY SIGHT. But Betterton said, if the text was to be disturbed, he saw no reason why a word might not be changed as well as a letter, and, instead of "put out thy light," you may read "put out thy eyes." At last it was agreed on all sides to refer the matter to the decision of Shakespeare himself, who delivered his sentiments as follows: "Faith, gentlemen, it is so long since I wrote the line, I have forgot my meaning. This I know, could I have dreamed so much nonsense would have been talked and writ about it, I would have blotted it out of my works; for I am sure, if any of these be my meaning, it doth me very little honor."

He was then interrogated concerning some other ambiguous passages in his works; but he declined any satisfactory answer; saying, if Mr. Theobald had not writ about it sufficiently, there were three or four more new editions of his plays coming out, which he hoped would satisfy every one: concluding, "I marvel nothing so much as that men will gird themselves at discovering obscure beauties in an author. Certes the greatest and most pregnant beauties are ever the plainest and most evidently striking; and when two meanings of a passage can in the least balance our judgments which to prefer, I hold it matter of unquestionable certainty that neither of them is worth a farthing." From his works our conversation turned on his monument; upon which, Shakespeare, shaking his sides, and addressing himself to Milton, cried out, "On my word, brother Milton, they have brought a noble set of poets together; they would have been hanged erst have [ere they had] convened such a company at their tables when alive." "True, brother," answered Milton, "unless we had been as incapable of eating then as we are now."

CHAPTER IX

More adventures in Elysium.

A crowd of spirits now joined us, whom I soon perceived to be the heroes, who here frequently pay their respects to the several bards the recorders of their actions. I now saw Achilles and Ulysses addressing themselves to Homer, and Aeneas and Julius Caesar to Virgil: Adam went up to Milton, upon which I whispered Mr. Dryden that I thought the devil should have paid his compliments there, according to his opinion. Dryden only answered, "I believe the devil was in me when I said so." Several applied themselves to Shakespeare, amongst whom Henry V made a very distinguishing appearance. While my eyes were fixed on that monarch a very small spirit came up to me, shook me heartily by the hand, and told me his name was THOMAS THUMB. I expressed great satisfaction in seeing him, nor could I help speaking my resentment against the historian, who had done such injustice to the stature of this great little man, which he represented to be no bigger than a span, whereas I plainly perceived at first sight he was full a foot and a half (and the 37th part of an inch more, as he himself informed me), being indeed little shorter than some considerable beaux of the present age. I asked this little hero concerning the truth of those stories related of him, viz., of the pudding, and the cow's belly. As to the former, he said it was a ridiculous legend, worthy to be laughed at; but as to the latter, he could not help owning there was some truth in it: nor had he any reason to be ashamed of it, as he was swallowed by surprise; adding, with great fierceness, that if he had had any weapon in his hand the cow should have as soon swallowed the devil.

He spoke the last word with so much fury, and seemed so confounded, that, perceiving the effect it had on him, I immediately waived the story, and, passing to other matters, we had much conversation touching giants. He said, so far from killing any, he had never seen one alive; that he believed those actions were by mistake recorded of him, instead of Jack the giant-killer, whom he knew very well, and who had, he fancied, extirpated the race. I assured him to the contrary, and told him I had myself seen a huge tame giant, who very complacently stayed in London a whole winter, at the special request of several gentlemen and ladies; though the affairs of his family called him home to Sweden.

I now beheld a stern-looking spirit leaning on the shoulder of another spirit, and presently discerned the former to be Oliver Cromwell, and the latter Charles Martel. I own I was a little surprised at seeing Cromwell here, for I had been taught by my grandmother that he was carried away by the devil himself in a tempest; but he assured me, on his honor, there was not the least truth in that story. However, he confessed he had narrowly escaped the bottomless pit; and, if the former part of his conduct had not been more to his honor than the latter, he had been certainly soused into it. He was, nevertheless, sent back to the upper world with this lot: ARMY, CAVALIER, DISTRESS.

He was born, for the second time, the day of Charles II's restoration, into a family which had lost a very considerable fortune in the service of that prince and his father, for which they received the reward very often conferred by princes on real merit, viz. 000. At 16 his father bought a small commission for him in the army, in which he served without any promotion all the reigns of Charles II and of his brother. At the Revolution he quitted his regiment, and followed the fortunes of his former master, and was in his service dangerously wounded at the famous battle of the Boyne, where he fought in the capacity of a private soldier. He recovered of this wound, and retired after the unfortunate king to Paris, where he was reduced to support a wife and seven children (for his lot had horns in it) by cleaning shoes and snuffing candles at the opera. In which situation, after he had spent a few miserable years, he died half-starved and broken-hearted. He then revisited Minos, who, compassionating his sufferings by means of that family, to whom he had been in his former capacity so bitter an enemy, suffered him to enter here.

My curiosity would not refrain asking him one question, i. e., whether in reality he had any desire to obtain the crown? He smiled, and said, "No more than an ecclesiastic hath to the miter, when he cries Nolo episcopari." Indeed, he seemed to express some contempt at the question, and presently turned away.

A venerable spirit appeared next, whom I found to be the great historian Livy. Alexander the Great, who was just arrived from the palace of death, passed by him with a frown. The historian, observing it, said, "Ay, you may frown; but those troops which conquered the base Asiatic slaves would have made no figure against the Romans." We then privately lamented the loss of the most valuable part of his history; after which he took occasion to commend the judicious collection made by Mr. Hook, which, he said, was infinitely preferable to all others; and at my mentioning Echard's he gave a bounce, not unlike the going off of a squib, and was departing from me, when I begged him to satisfy my curiosity in one point, whether he was really superstitious or no? For I had always believed he was till Mr. Leibnitz had assured me to the contrary. He answered sullenly, "Doth Mr. Leibnitz know my mind better than myself?" and then walked away.

CHAPTER X

The author is surprised at meeting Julian the apostate in Elysium; but is satisfied by him by what means he procured his entrance there. Julian relates his adventures in the character of a slave.

As he was departing I heard him salute a spirit by the name of Mr. Julian the apostate. This exceedingly amazed me; for I had concluded that no man ever had a better title to the bottomless pit than he. But I soon found that this same Julian the apostate was also the very individual archbishop Latimer. He told me that several lies had been raised on him in his former capacity, nor was he so bad a man as he had been represented. However, he had been denied admittance, and forced to undergo several subsequent pilgrimages on earth, and to act in the different characters of a slave, a Jew, a general, an heir, a carpenter, a beau, a monk, a fiddler, a wise man, a king, a fool, a beggar, a prince, a statesman, a soldier, a tailor, an alderman, a poet, a knight, a dancing-master, and three times a bishop, before his martyrdom, which, together with his other behavior in this last character, satisfied the judge, and procured him a passage to the blessed regions.

I told him such various characters must have produced incidents extremely entertaining; and if he remembered all, as I supposed he did, and had leisure, I should be obliged to him for the recital. He answered he perfectly recollected every circumstance; and as to leisure, the only business of that happy place was to contribute to the happiness of each other. He therefore thanked me for adding to his, in proposing to him a method of increasing mine. I then took my little darling in one hand, and my favorite fellow-traveler in the other, and, going with him to a sunny bank of flowers, we all sat down, and he began as follows: "I suppose you are sufficiently acquainted with my story during the time I acted the part of the emperor Julian, though I assure you all which hath been related of me is not true, particularly with regard to the many prodigies forerunning my death. However, they are now very little worth disputing; and if they can serve any purpose of the historian they are extremely at his service. My next entrance into the world was at Laodicea, in Syria, in a Roman family of no great note; and, being of a roving disposition, I came at the age of seventeen to Constantinople, where, after about a year's stay, I set out for Thrace, at the time when the emperor Valens admitted the Goths into that country. I was there so captivated with the beauty of a Gothic lady, the wife of one Rodoric, a captain, whose name, out of the most delicate tenderness for her lovely sex, I shall even at this distance conceal; since her behavior to me was more consistent with good-nature than with that virtue which women are obliged to preserve against every assailant. In order to procure an intimacy with this woman I sold myself a slave to her husband, who, being of a nation not over-inclined to jealousy, presented me to his wife, for those very reasons which would have induced one of a jealous complexion to have withheld me from her, namely, for that I was young and handsome.

"Matters succeeded so far according to my wish, and the sequel answered those hopes which this beginning had raised. I soon perceived my service was very acceptable to her; I often met her eyes, nor did she withdraw them without a confusion which is scarce consistent with entire purity of heart. Indeed, she gave me every day fresh encouragement; but the unhappy distance which circumstances had placed between us deterred me long from making any direct attack; and she was too strict an observer of decorum to violate the severe rules of modesty by advancing first; but passion at last got the better of my respect, and I resolved to make one bold attempt, whatever was the consequence. Accordingly, laying hold of the first kind opportunity, when she was alone and my master abroad, I stoutly assailed the citadel and carried it by storm. Well may I say by storm; for the resistance I met was extremely resolute, and indeed as much as the most perfect decency would require. She swore often she would cry out for help; but I answered it was in vain, seeing there was no person near to assist her; and probably she believed me, for she did not once actually cry out, which if she had, I might very likely have been prevented.

"When she found her virtue thus subdued against her will she patiently submitted to her fate, and quietly suffered me a long time to enjoy the most delicious fruits of my victory; but envious fortune resolved to make me pay a dear price for my pleasure. One day in the midst of our happiness we were suddenly surprised by the unexpected return of her husband, who, coming directly into his wife's apartment, just allowed me time to creep under the bed. The disorder in which he found his wife might have surprised a jealous temper; but his was so far otherwise, that possibly no mischief might have happened had he not by a cross accident discovered my legs, which were not well hid. He immediately drew me out by them, and then, turning to his wife with a stern countenance, began to handle a weapon he wore by his side, with which I am persuaded he would have instantly dispatched her, had I not very gallantly, and with many imprecations, asserted her innocence and my own guilt; which, however, I protested had hitherto gone no farther than design. She so well seconded my plea (for she was a woman of wonderful art), that he was at length imposed upon; and now all his rage was directed against me, threatening all manner of tortures, which the poor lady was in too great a fright and confusion to dissuade him from executing; and perhaps, if her concern for me had made her attempt it, it would have raised a jealousy in him not afterwards to be removed.

"After some hesitation Roderic cried out he had luckily hit on the most proper punishment for me in the world, by a method which would at once do severe justice on me for my criminal intention, and at the same time prevent me from any danger of executing my wicked purpose hereafter. This cruel resolution was immediately executed, and I was no longer worthy the name of a man.

"Having thus disqualified me from doing him any future injury, he still retained me in his family; but the lady, very probably repenting of what she had done, and looking on me as the author of her guilt, would never for the future give me either a kind word or look: and shortly after, a great exchange being made between the Romans and the Goths of dogs for men, my lady exchanged me with a Roman widow for a small lap-dog, giving a considerable sum of money to boot.

"In this widow's service I remained seven years, during all which time I was very barbarously treated. I was worked without the least mercy, and often severely beat by a swinging maid-servant, who never called me by any other names than those of the Thing and the Animal. Though I used my utmost industry to please, it never was in my power. Neither the lady nor her woman would eat anything I touched, saying they did not believe me wholesome. It is unnecessary to repeat particulars; in a word, you can imagine no kind of ill usage which I did not suffer in this family.

"At last an heathen priest, an acquaintance of my lady's, obtained me of her for a present. The scene was now totally changed, and I had as much reason to be satisfied with my present situation as I had to lament my former. I was so absolutely my master's favorite, that the rest of the slaves paid me almost as much regard as they showed to him, well knowing that it was entirely in my power to command and treat them as I pleased. I was intrusted with all my master's secrets, and used to assist him in privately conveying away by night the sacrifices from the altars, which the people believed the deities themselves devoured. Upon these we feasted very elegantly, nor could invention suggest a rarity which we did not pamper ourselves with. Perhaps you may admire at the close union between this priest and his slave, but we lived in an intimacy which the Christians thought criminal; but my master, who knew the will of the gods, with whom he told me he often conversed, assured me it was perfectly innocent.

"This happy life continued about four years, when my master's death, occasioned by a surfeit got by overfeeding on several exquisite dainties, put an end to it.

"I now fell into the hands of one of a very different disposition, and this was no other than the celebrated St. Chrysostom, who dieted me with sermons instead of sacrifices, and filled my ears with good things, but not my belly. Instead of high food to fatten and pamper my flesh, I had receipts to mortify and reduce it. With these I edified so well, that within a few months I became a skeleton. However, as he had converted me to his faith, I was well enough satisfied with this new manner of living, by which he taught me I might insure myself an eternal reward in a future state. The saint was a good-natured man, and never gave me an ill word but once, which was occasioned by my neglecting to place Aristophanes, which was his constant bedfellow, on his pillow. He was, indeed, extremely fond of that Greek poet, and frequently made me read his comedies to him. When I came to any of the loose passages he would smile, and say, 'It was pity his matter was not as pure as his style;' of which latter he was so immoderately fond that, notwithstanding the detestation he expressed for obscenity, he hath made me repeat those passages ten times over. The character of this good man hath been very unjustly attacked by his heathen contemporaries, particularly with regard to women; but his severe invectives against that sex are his sufficient justification.

"From the service of this saint, from whom I received manumission, I entered into the family of Timasius, a leader of great eminence in the imperial army, into whose favor I so far insinuated myself that he preferred me to a good command, and soon made me partaker of both his company and his secrets. I soon grew intoxicated with this preferment, and the more he loaded me with benefits the more he raised my opinion of my own merit, which, still outstripping the rewards he conferred on me, inspired me rather with dissatisfaction than gratitude. And thus, by preferring me beyond my merit or first expectation, he made me an envious aspiring enemy, whom perhaps a more moderate bounty would have preserved a dutiful servant.

"I fell now acquainted with one Lucilius, a creature of the prime minister Eutropius, who had by his favor been raised to the post of a tribune; a man of low morals, and eminent only in that meanest of qualities, cunning. This gentleman, imagining me a fit tool for the minister's purpose, having often sounded my principles of honor and honesty, both which he declared to me were words without meaning, and finding my ready concurrence in his sentiments, recommended me to Eutropius as very proper to execute some wicked purposes he had contrived against my frend Timasius. The minister embraced this recommendation, and I was accordingly acquainted by Lucilius (after some previous accounts of the great esteem Eutropius entertained of me, from the testimony he had borne of my parts) that he would introduce me to him; adding that he was a great encourager of merit, and that I might depend upon his favor.

"I was with little difficulty prevailed on to accept of this invitation. A late hour therefore the next evening being appointed, I attended my friend Lucilius to the minister's house.

"He received me with the utmost civility and cheerfulness, and affected so much regard to me, that I, who knew nothing of these high scenes of life, concluded I had in him a most disinterested friend, owing to the favorable report which Lucilius had made of me. I was however soon cured of this opinion; for immediately after supper our discourse turned on the injustice which the generality of the world were guilty of in their conduct to great men, expecting that they should reward their private merit, without ever endeavoring to apply it to their use. 'What avail,' said Eutropius, 'the learning, wit, courage, or any virtue which a man may be possessed of, to me, unless I receive some benefit from them? Hath he not more merit to me who doth my business and obeys my commands, without any of these qualities?' I gave such entire satisfaction in my answers on this head, that both the minister and his creature grew bolder, and after some preface began to accuse Timasius. At last, finding I did not attempt to defend him, Lucilius swore a great oath that he was not fit to live, and that he would destroy him. Eutropius answered that it would be too dangerous a task: 'Indeed,' says he, 'his crimes are of so black a dye, and so well known to the emperor, that his death must be a very acceptable service, and could not fail meeting a proper reward: but I question whether you are capable of executing it.' 'If he is not,' cried I, 'I am; and surely no man can have greater motives to destroy him than myself: for, besides his disloyalty to my prince, for whom I have so perfect a duty, I have private disobligations to him. I have had fellows put over my head, to the great scandal of the service in general, and to my own prejudice and disappointment in particular.' I will not repeat you my whole speech; but, to be as concise as possible, when we parted that evening the minister squeezed me heartily by the hand, and with great commendation of my honesty and assurances of his favor, he appointed me the next evening to come to him alone; when, finding me, after a little more scrutiny, ready for his purpose, he proposed to me to accuse Timasius of high treason, promising me the highest rewards if I would undertake it. The consequence to him, I suppose you know, was ruin; but what was it to me? Why, truly, when I waited on Eutropius for the fulfilling his promises, received me with great distance and coldness; and, on my dropping some hints of my expectations from him, he affected not to understand me; saying he thought impunity was the utmost I could hope for on discovering my accomplice, whose offense was only greater than mine, as he was in a higher station; and telling me he had great difficulty to obtain a pardon for me from the emperor, which he said, he had struggled very hardly for, as he had worked the discovery out of me. He turned away, and addressed himself to another person.

"I was so incensed at this treatment, that I resolved revenge, and should certainly have pursued it, had he not cautiously prevented me by taking effectual means to despatch me soon after out of the world.

"You will, I believe, now think I had a second good chance for the bottomless pit, and indeed Minos seemed inclined to tumble me in, till he was informed of the revenge taken on me by Roderic, and my seven years' subsequent servitude to the widow; which he thought sufficient to make atonement for all the crimes a single life could admit of, and so sent me back to try my fortune a third time."

CHAPTER XI

In which Julian relates his adventures in the character of an avaricious Jew.

"The next character in which I was destined to appear in the flesh was that of an avaricious Jew. I was born in Alexandria in Egypt. My name was Balthazar. Nothing very remarkable happened to me till the year of the memorable tumult in which the Jews of that city are reported in history to have massacred more Christians than at that time dwelt in it. Indeed, the truth is, they did maul the dogs pretty handsomely; but I myself was not present, for as all our people were ordered to be armed, I took that opportunity of selling two swords, which probably I might otherwise never have disposed of, they being extremely old and rusty; so that, having no weapon left, I did not care to venture abroad. Besides, though I really thought it an act meriting salvation to murder the Nazarenes, as the fact was to be committed at midnight, at which time, to avoid suspicion, we were all to sally from our own houses, I could not persuade myself to consume so much oil in sitting up to that hour: for these reasons therefore I remained at home that evening.

"I was at this time greatly enamored with one Hypatia, the daughter of a philosopher; a young lady of the greatest beauty and merit: indeed, she had every imaginable ornament both of mind and body. She seemed not to dislike my person; but there were two obstructions to our marriage, viz., my religion and her poverty: both which might probably have been got over, had not those dogs the Christians murdered her; and, what is worse, afterwards burned her body: worse, I say, because I lost by that means a jewel of some value, which I had presented to her, designing, if our nuptials did not take place, to demand it of her back again.

"Being thus disappointed in my love, I soon after left Alexandria and went to the imperial city, where I apprehended I should find a good market for jewels on the approaching marriage of the emperor with Athenais. I disguised myself as a beggar on this journey, for these reasons: first, as I imagined I should thus carry my jewels with greater safety; and, secondly, to lessen my expenses; which latter expedient succeeded so well, that I begged two oboli on my way more than my traveling cost me, my diet being chiefly roots, and my drink water.

"But perhaps, it had been better for me if I had been more lavish and more expeditious; for the ceremony was over before I reached Constantinople; so that I lost that glorious opportunity of disposing of my jewels with which many of our people were greatly enriched.

"The life of a miser is very little worth relating, as it is one constant scheme of getting or saving money. I shall therefore repeat to you some few only of my adventures, without regard to any order.

"A Roman Jew, who was a great lover of Falernian wine, and who indulged himself very freely with it, came to dine at my house; when, knowing he should meet with little wine, and that of the cheaper sort, sent me in half-a-dozen jars of Falernian. Can you believe I would not give this man his own wine? Sir, I adulterated it so that I made six jars of [them] three, which he and his friend drank; the other three I afterwards sold to the very person who originally sent them me, knowing he would give a better price than any other.

"A noble Roman came one day to my house in the country, which I had purchased, for half the value, of a distressed person. My neighbors paid him the compliment of some music, on which account, when he departed, he left a piece of gold with me to be distributed among them. I pocketed this money, and ordered them a small vessel of sour wine, which I could not have sold for above two drachms, and afterwards made them pay in work three times the value of it.

"As I was not entirely void of religion, though I pretended to infinitely more than I had, so I endeavored to reconcile my transactions to my conscience as well as possible. Thus I never invited any one to eat with me, but those on whose pockets I had some design. After our collation it was constantly my method to set down in a book I kept for that purpose, what I thought they owed me for their meal. Indeed, this was generally a hundred times as much as they could have dined elsewhere for; but, however, it was quid pro quo, if not ad valorem. Now, whenever the opportunity offered of imposing on them I considered it only as paying myself what they owed me: indeed, I did not always confine myself strictly to what I had set down, however extravagant that was; but I reconciled taking the overplus to myself as usance.

"But I was not only too cunning for others, I sometimes overreached myself. I have contracted distempers for want of food and warmth, which have put me to the expense of a physician; nay, I once very narrowly escaped death by taking bad drugs, only to save one seven-eighth per cent in the price.

"By these and such like means, in the midst of poverty and every kind of distress, I saw myself master of an immense fortune, the casting up and ruminating on which was my daily and only pleasure. This was, however, obstructed and embittered by two considerations, which against my will often invaded my thoughts. One, which would have been intolerable (but that indeed seldom troubled me), was, that I must one day leave my darling treasure.

"The other haunted me continually, viz., that my riches were no greater. However, I comforted myself against this reflection by an assurance that they would increase daily: on which head my hopes were so extensive that I may say with Virgil -

'His ego nec metas rerum nec tempora pono.'

Indeed I am convinced that, had I possessed the whole globe of earth, save one single drachma, which I had been certain never to be master of, I am convinced, I say, that single drachma would have given me more uneasiness than all the rest could afford me pleasure.

"To say the truth, between my solicitude in contriving schemes to procure money and my extreme anxiety in preserving it, I never had one moment of ease while awake nor of quiet when in my sleep.

"In all the characters through which I have passed, I have never undergone half the misery I suffered in this; and, indeed, Minos seemed to be of the same opinion; for while I stood trembling and shaking in expectation of my sentence he bid me go back about my business, for that nobody was to be damn'd in more worlds than one. And, indeed, I have since learned that the devil will not receive a miser."

CHAPTER XII

What happened to Julian in the characters of a general, an heir, a carpenter, and a beau.

"The next step I took into the world was at Apollonia, in Thrace, where I was born of a beautiful Greek slave, who was the mistress of Eutyches, a great favorite of the emperor Zeno. That prince, at his restoration, gave me the command of a cohort, I being then but fifteen years of age; and a little afterwards, before I had even seen an army, preferred me, over the heads of all the old officers, to be a tribune.

"As I found an easy access to the emperor, by means of my father's intimacy with him, he being a very good courtier, or, in other words, a most prostitute flatterer, so I soon ingratiated myself with Zeno, and so well imitated my father in flattering him, that he would never part with me from about his person. So that the first armed force I ever beheld was that with which Marcian surrounded the palace, where I was then shut up with the rest of the court.

"I was afterwards put at the head of a legion and ordered to march into Syria with Theodoric the Goth; that is, I mean my legion was so ordered; for, as to myself, I remained at court, with the name and pay of a general, without the labor or the danger.

"As nothing could be more gay, i. e., debauched, than Zeno's court, so the ladies of gay disposition had great sway in it; particularly one, whose name was Fausta, who, though not extremely handsome, was by her wit and sprightliness very agreeable to the emperor. With her I lived in good correspondence, and we together disposed of all kinds of commissions in the army, not to those who had most merit, but who would purchase at the highest rate. My levee was now prodigiously thronged by officers who returned from the campaigns, who, though they might have been convinced by daily example how ineffectual a recommendation their services were, still continued indefatigable in attendance, and behaved to me with as much observance and respect as I should have been entitled to for making their fortunes, while I suffered them and their families to starve.

"Several poets, likewise, addressed verses to me, in which they celebrated my achievements; and what, perhaps, may seem strange to us at present, I received all this incense with most greedy vanity, without once reflecting that, as I did not deserve these compliments, they should rather put me in mind of my defects.

"My father was now dead, and I became so absolute in the emperor's grace that one unacquainted with courts would scarce believe the servility with which all kinds of persons who entered the walls of the palace behaved towards me. A bow, a smile, a nod from me, as I passed through cringing crowds, were esteemed as signal favors; but a gracious word made any one happy; and, indeed, had this real benefit attending it, that it drew on the person on whom it was bestowed a very great degree of respect from all others; for these are of current value in courts, and, like notes in trading communities, are assignable from one to the other. The smile of a court favorite immediately raises the person who receives it, and gives a value to his smile when conferred on an inferior: thus the smile is transferred from one to the other, and the great man at last is the person to discount it. For instance, a very low fellow hath a desire for a place. To whom is he to apply? Not to the great man; for to him he hath no access. He therefore applies to A, who is the creature of B, who is the tool of C, who is the flatterer of D, who is the catamite of E, who is the pimp of F, who is the bully of G, who is the buffoon of I, who is the husband of K, who is the whore of L, who is the bastard of M, who is the instrument of the great man. Thus the smile descending regularly from the great man to A, is discounted back again, and at last paid by the great man.

"It is manifest that a court would subsist as difficultly without this kind of coin as a trading city without paper credit. Indeed, they differ in this, that their value is not quite so certain, and a favorite may protest his smile without the danger of bankruptcy.

"In the midst of all this glory the emperor died, and Anastasius was preferred to the crown. As it was yet uncertain whether I should not continue in favor, I was received as usual at my entrance into the palace to pay my respects to the new emperor; but I was no sooner rumped by him than I received the same compliment from all the rest; the whole room, like a regiment of soldiers, turning their backs to me all at once: my smile now was become of equal value with the note of a broken banker, and every one was as cautious not to receive it.

"I made as much haste as possible from the court, and shortly after from the city, retreating to the place of my nativity, where I spent the remainder of my days in a retired life in husbandry, the only amusement for which I was qualified, having neither learning nor virtue.

"When I came to the gate Minos again seemed at first doubtful, but at length dismissed me; saying though I had been guilty of many heinous crimes, in as much as I had, though a general, never been concerned in spilling human blood, I might return again to earth.

"I was now again born in Alexandria, and, by great accident, entering into the womb of my daughter-in-law, came forth my own grandson, inheriting that fortune which I had before amassed.

"Extravagance was now as notoriously my vice as avarice had been formerly; and I spent in a very short life what had cost me the labor of a very long one to rake together. Perhaps you will think my present condition was more to be envied than my former: but upon my word it was very little so; for, by possessing everything almost before I desired it, I could hardly ever say I enjoyed my wish: I scarce ever knew the delight of satisfying a craving appetite. Besides, as I never once thought, my mind was useless to me, and I was an absolute stranger to all the pleasures arising from it. Nor, indeed, did my education qualify me for any delicacy in other enjoyments; so that in the midst of plenty I loathed everything. Taste for elegance I had none; and the greatest of corporeal blisses I felt no more from than the lowest animal. In a word, as while a miser I had plenty without daring to use it, so now I had it without appetite.

"But if I was not very happy in the height of my enjoyment, so I afterwards became perfectly miserable; being soon overtaken by disease, and reduced to distress, till at length, with a broken constitution and broken heart, I ended my wretched days in a jail: nor can I think the sentence of Minos too mild, who condemned me, after having taken a large dose of avarice, to wander three years on the banks of Cocytus, with the knowledge of having spent the fortune in the person of the grandson which I had raised in that of the grandfather.

"The place of my birth, on my return to the world, was Constantinople, where my father was a carpenter. The first thing I remember was, the triumph of Belisarius, which was, indeed, most noble show; but nothing pleased me so much as the figure of Gelimer, king of the African Vandals, who, being led captive on this occasion, reflecting with disdain on the mutation of his own fortune, and on the ridiculous empty pomp of the conqueror, cried out, VANITY, VANITY, ALL IS MERE VANITY.'

"I was bred up to my father's trade, and you may easily believe so low a sphere could produce no adventures worth your notice. However, I married a woman I liked, and who proved a very tolerable wife. My days were passed in hard labor, but this procured me health, and I enjoyed a homely supper at night with my wife with more pleasure than I apprehend greater persons find at their luxurious meals. My life had scarce any variety in it, and at my death I advanced to Minos with great confidence of entering the gate: but I was unhappily obliged to discover some frauds I had been guilty of in the measure of my work when I worked by the foot, as well as my laziness when I was employed by the day. On which account, when I attempted to pass, the angry judge laid hold on me by the shoulders, and turned me back so violently, that, had I had a neck of flesh and bone, I believe he would have broke it."

CHAPTER XIII

Julian passes into a fop.

"My scene of action was Rome. I was born into a noble family, and heir to a considerable fortune. On which my parents, thinking I should not want any talents, resolved very kindly and wisely to throw none away upon me. The only instructors of my youth were therefore one Saltator, who taught me several motions for my legs; and one Ficus, whose business was to show me the cleanest way (as he called it) of cutting off a man's head. When I was well accomplished in these sciences, I thought nothing more wanting, but what was to be furnished by the several mechanics in Rome, who dealt in dressing and adorning the pope. Being therefore well equipped with all which their art could produce, I became at the age of twenty a complete finished beau. And now during forty-five years I dressed, I sang and danced, and danced and sang, I bowed and ogled, and ogled and bowed, till, in the sixty-sixth year of my age, I got cold by overheating myself with dancing, and died.

"Minos told me, as I was unworthy of Elysium, so I was too insignificant to be damned, and therefore bade me walk back again."

CHAPTER XIV

Adventures in the person of a monk.

"Fortune now placed me in the character of a younger brother of a good house, and I was in my youth sent to school; but learning was now at so low an ebb, that my master himself could hardly construe a sentence of Latin; and as for Greek, he could not read it. With very little knowledge therefore, and with altogether as little virtue, I was set apart for the church, and at the proper age commenced monk. I lived many years retired in a cell, a life very agreeable to the gloominess of my temper, which was much inclined to despise the world; that is, in other words, to envy all men of superior fortune and qualifications, and in general to hate and detest the human species. Notwithstanding which, I could, on proper occasions, submit to flatter the vilest fellow in nature, which I did one Stephen, a eunuch, a favorite of the emperor Justinian II, one of the wickedest wretches whom perhaps the world ever saw. I not only wrote a panegyric on this man, but I commended him as a pattern to all others in my sermons; by which means I so greatly ingratiated myself with him, that he introduced me to the emperor's presence, where I prevailed so far by the same methods, that I was shortly taken from my cell, and preferred to a place at court. I was no sooner established in the favor of Justinian than I prompted him to all kind of cruelty. As I was of a sour morose temper, and hated nothing more than the symptoms of happiness appearing in any countenance, I represented all kind of diversion and amusement as the most horrid sins. I inveighed against cheerfulness as levity, and encouraged nothing but gravity, or, to confess the truth to you, hypocrisy. The unhappy emperor followed my advice, and incensed the people by such repeated barbarities, that he was at last deposed by them and banished.

"I now retired again to my cell (for historians mistake in saying I was put to death), where I remained safe from the danger of the irritated mob, whom I cursed in my own heart as much as they could curse me.

"Justinian, after three years of his banishment, returned to Constantinople in disguise, and paid me a visit. I at first affected not to know him, and without the least compunction of gratitude for his former favors, intended not to receive him, till a thought immediately suggested itself to me how I might convert him to my advantage, I pretended to recollect him; and, blaming the shortness of my memory and badness of my eyes, I sprung forward and embraced him with great affection.

"My design was to betray him to Apsimar, who, I doubted not, would generously reward such a service. I therefore very earnestly requested him to spend the whole evening with me; to which he consented. I formed an excuse for leaving him a few minutes, and ran away to the palace to acquaint Apsimar with the guest whom I had then in my cell. He presently ordered a guard to go with me and seize him; but, whether the length of my stay gave him any suspicion, or whether he changed his purpose after my departure, I know not; for at my return we found he had given us the slip; nor could we with the most diligent search discover him.

"Apsimar, being disappointed of his prey, now raged at me; at first denouncing the most dreadful vengeance if I did not produce the deposed monarch. However, by soothing his passion when at the highest, and afterwards by canting and flattery, I made a shift to escape his fury.

"When Justinian was restored I very confidently went to wish him joy of his restoration: but it seems he had unfortunately heard of my treachery, so that he at first received me coldly, and afterwards upbraided me openly with what I had done. I persevered stoutly in denying it, as I knew no evidence could be produced against me; till, finding him irreconcilable, I betook myself to reviling him in my sermons, and on every other occasion, as an enemy to the church and good men, and as an infidel, a heretic, an atheist, a heathen, and an Arian. This I did immediately on his return, and before he gave those flagrant proofs of his inhumanity which afterwards sufficiently verified all I had said.

"Luckily I died on the same day when a great number of those forces which Justinian had sent against the Thracian Bosphorus, and who had executed such unheard-of cruelties there, perished. As every one of these was cast into the bottomless pit, Minos was so tired with condemnation, that he proclaimed that all present who had not been concerned in that bloody expedition might, if they pleased, return to the other world. I took him at his word, and, presently turning about, began my journey."

CHAPTER XV

Julian passes into the character of a fiddler.

"Rome was now the seat of my nativity. My mother was an African, a woman of no great beauty, but a favorite, I suppose from her piety, of pope Gregory II. Who was my father I know not, but I believe no very considerable man; for after the death of that pope, who was, out of his religion, a very good friend of my mother, we fell into great distress, and were at length reduced to walk the streets of Rome; nor had either of us any other support but a fiddle, on which I played with pretty tolerable skill; for, as my genius turned naturally to music, so I had been in my youth very early instructed at the expense of the good pope. This afforded us but a very poor livelihood: for, though I had often a numerous crowd of hearers, few ever thought themselves obliged to contribute the smallest pittance to the poor starving wretch who had given them pleasure. Nay, some of the graver sort, after an hour's attention to my music, have gone away shaking their heads, and crying it was a shame such vagabonds were suffered to stay in the city.

"To say the truth, I am confident the fiddle would not have kept us alive had we entirely depended on the generosity of my hearers. My mother therefore was forced to use her own industry; and while I was soothing the ears of the crowd, she applied to their pockets, and that generally with such good success that we now began to enjoy a very comfortable subsistence; and indeed, had we had the least prudence or forecast, might have soon acquired enough to enable us to quit this dangerous and dishonorable way of life: but I know not what is the reason that money got with labor and safety is constantly preserved, while the produce of danger and ease is commonly spent as easily, and often as wickedly, as acquired. Thus we proportioned our expenses rather by what we had than what we wanted or even desired; and on obtaining a considerable booty we have even forced nature into the most profligate extravagance, and have been wicked without inclination.

"We carried on this method of thievery for a long time without detection: but, as Fortune generally leaves persons of extraordinary ingenuity in the lurch at last, so did she us; for my poor mother was taken in the fact, and, together with myself, as her accomplice, hurried before a magistrate.

"Luckily for us, the person who was to be our judge was the greatest lover of music in the whole city, and had often sent for me to play to him, for which, as he had given me very small rewards, perhaps his gratitude now moved him: but, whatever was his motive, he browbeat the informers against us, and treated their evidence with so little favor, that their mouths were soon stopped, and we dismissed with honor; acquitted, I should rather have it said, for we were not suffered to depart till I had given the judge several tunes on the fiddle.

"We escaped the better on this occasion because the person robbed happened to be a poet; which gave the judge, who was a facetious person, many opportunities of jesting. He said poets and musicians should agree together, seeing they had married sisters; which he afterwards explained to be the sister arts. And when the piece of gold was produced he burst into a loud laugh, and said it must be the golden age, when poets had gold in their pockets, and in that age there could be no robbers. He made many more jests of the same kind, but a small taste will suffice.

"It is a common saying that men should take warning by any signal delivery; but I cannot approve the justice of it; for to me it seems that the acquittal of a guilty person should rather inspire him with confidence, and it had this effect on us: for we now laughed at the law, and despised its punishments, which we found were to be escaped even against positive evidence. We imagined the late example was rather a warning to the accuser than the criminal, and accordingly proceeded in the most impudent and flagitious manner.

"Among other robberies, one night, being admitted by the servants into the house of an opulent priest, my mother took an opportunity, whilst the servants were dancing to my tunes, to convey away a silver vessel; this she did without the least sacrilegious intention; but it seems the cup, which was a pretty large one, was dedicated to holy uses, and only borrowed by the priest on an entertainment which he made for some of his brethren. We were immediately pursued upon this robbery (the cup being taken in our possession), and carried before the same magistrate, who had before behaved to us with so much gentleness: but his countenance was now changed, for the moment the priest appeared against us, his severity was as remarkable as his candor had been before, and we were both ordered to be stripped and whipped through the streets.

"This sentence was executed with great severity, the priest himself attending and encouraging the executioner, which he said he did for the good of our souls; but, though our backs were both flayed, neither my mother's torments nor my own afflicted me so much as the indignity offered to my poor fiddle, which was carried in triumph before me, and treated with a contempt by the multitude, intimating a great scorn for the science I had the honor to profess; which, as it is one of the noblest inventions of men, and as I had been always in the highest degree proud of my excellence in it, I suffered so much from the ill-treatment my fiddle received, that I would have given all my remainder of skin to have preserved it from this affront.

"My mother survived the whipping a very short time; and I was now reduced to great distress and misery, till a young Roman of considerable rank took a fancy to me, received me into his family, and conversed with me in the utmost familiarity. He had a violent attachment to music, and would learn to play on the fiddle; but, through want of genius for the science, he never made any considerable progress. However, I flattered his performance, and he grew extravagantly fond of me for so doing. Had I continued this behavior I might possibly have reaped the greatest advantages from his kindness; but I had raised his own opinion of his musical abilities so high, that he now began to prefer his skill to mine, a presumption I could not bear. One day as we were playing in concert he was horribly out; nor was it possible, as he destroyed the harmony, to avoid telling him of it. Instead of receiving my correction, he answered it was my blunder and not his, and that I had mistaken the key. Such an affront from my own scholar was beyond human patience; I flew into a violent passion, I flung down my instrument in a rage, and swore I was not to be taught music at my age. He answered, with as much warmth, nor was he to be instructed by a strolling fiddler. The dispute ended in a challenge to play a prize before judges. This wager was determined in my favor; but the purchase was a dear one, for I lost my friend by it, who now, twitting me with all his kindness, with my former ignominious punishment, and the destitute condition from which I had been by his bounty relieved, discarded me for ever.

"While I lived with this gentleman I became known, among others, to Sabina, a lady of distinction, and who valued herself much on her taste for music. She no sooner heard of my being discarded than she took me into her house, where I was extremely well clothed and fed. Notwithstanding which, my situation was far from agreeable; for I was obliged to submit to her constant reprehensions before company, which gave me the greater uneasiness because they were always wrong; nor am I certain that she did not by these provocations contribute to my death: for, as experience had taught me to give up my resentment to my bread, so my passions, for want of outward vent, preyed inwardly on my vitals, and perhaps occasioned the distemper of which I sickened.

"The lady, who, amidst all the faults she found, was very fond of me, nay, probably was the fonder of me the more faults she found, immediately called in the aid of three celebrated physicians. The doctors (being well fee'd) made me seven visits in three days, and two of them were at the door to visit me the eighth time, when, being acquainted that I was just dead, they shook their heads and departed.

"When I came to Minos he asked me with a smile whether I had brought my fiddle with me; and, receiving an answer in the negative, he bid me get about my business, saying it was well for me that the devil was no lover of music."

CHAPTER XVI

The history of the wise man.

"I now returned to Rome, but in a very different character. Fortune had now allotted me a serious part to act. I had even in my infancy a grave disposition, nor was I ever seen to smile, which infused an opinion into all about me that I was a child of great solidity; some foreseeing that I should be a judge, and others a bishop. At two years old my father presented me with a rattle, which I broke to pieces with great indignation. This the good parent, being extremely wise, regarded as an eminent symptom of my wisdom, and cried out in a kind of ecstasy, 'Well said, boy! I warrant thou makest a great man.'

"At school I could never be persuaded to play with my mates; not that I spent my hours in learning, to which I was not in the least addicted, nor indeed had I any talents for it. However, the solemnity of my carriage won so much on my master, who was a most sagacious person, that I was his chief favorite, and my example on all occasions was recommended to the other boys, which filled them with envy, and me with pleasure; but, though they envied me, they all paid me that involuntary respect which it is the curse attending this passion to bear towards its object.

"I had now obtained universally the character of a very wise young man, which I did not altogether purchase without pains; for the restraint I laid on myself in abstaining from the several diversions adapted to my years cost me many a yearning; but the pride which I inwardly enjoyed in the fancied dignity of my character made me some amends.

"Thus I passed on, without anything very memorable happening to me, till I arrived at the age of twenty-three, when unfortunately I fell acquainted with a young Neapolitan lady whose name was Ariadne. Her beauty was so exquisite that her first sight made a violent impression on me; this was again improved by her behavior, which was most genteel, easy, and affable: lastly, her conversation completed the conquest. In this she discovered a strong and lively understanding, with the sweetest and most benign temper. This lovely creature was about eighteen when I first unhappily beheld her at Rome, on a visit to a relation with whom I had great intimacy. As our interviews at first were extremely frequent, my passions were captivated before I apprehended the least danger; and the sooner probably, as the young lady herself, to whom I consulted every method of recommendation, was not displeased with my being her admirer.

"Ariadne, having spent three months at Rome, now returned to Naples, bearing my heart with her: on the other hand, I had all the assurances consistent with the constraint under which the most perfect modesty lays a young woman, that her own heart was not entirely unaffected. I soon found her absence gave me an uneasiness not easy to be borne or to remove. I now first applied to diversions (of the graver sort, particularly to music), but in vain; they rather raised my desires and heightened my anguish. My passion at length grew so violent, that I began to think of satisfying it. As the first step to this, I cautiously inquired into the circumstances of Ariadne's parents, with which I was hitherto unacquainted: though, indeed, I did not apprehend they were extremely great, notwithstanding the handsome appearance of their daughter at Rome. Upon examination, her fortune exceeded my expectation, but was not sufficient to justify my marriage with her, in the opinion of the wise and prudent. I had now a violent struggle between wisdom and happiness, in which, after several grievous pangs, wisdom got the better. I could by no means prevail with myself to sacrifice that character of profound wisdom, which I had with such uniform conduct obtained, and with such caution hitherto preserved. I therefore resolved to conquer my affection, whatever it cost me; and indeed it did not cost me a little.

"While I was engaged in this conflict (for it lasted a long time) Ariadne returned to Rome: her presence was a terrible enemy to my wisdom, which even in her absence had with great difficulty stood its ground. It seems (as she hath since told me in Elysium with much merriment) I had made the same impressions on her which she had made on me. Indeed, I believe my wisdom would have been totally subdued by this surprise, had it not cunningly suggested to me a method of satisfying my passion without doing any injury to my reputation. This was by engaging her privately as a mistress, which was at that time reputable enough at Rome, provided the affair was managed with an air of slyness and gravity, though the secret was known to the whole city.

"I immediately set about this project, and employed every art and engine to effect it. I had particularly bribed her priest, and an old female acquaintance and distant relation of hers, into my interest: but all was in vain; her virtue opposed the passion in her breast as strongly as wisdom had opposed it in mine. She received my proposals with the utmost disdain, and presently refused to see or hear from me any more.

"She returned again to Naples, and left me in a worse condition than before. My days I now passed with the most irksome uneasiness, and my nights were restless and sleepless. The story of our amour was now pretty public, and the ladies talked of our match as certain; but my acquaintance denied their assent, saying, 'No, no, he is too wise to marry so imprudently.' This their opinion gave me, I own, very great pleasure; but, to say the truth, scarce compensated the pangs I suffered to preserve it.

"One day, while I was balancing with myself, and had almost resolved to enjoy my happiness at the price of my character, a friend brought me word that Ariadne was married. This news struck me to the soul; and though I had resolution enough to maintain my gravity before him (for which I suffered not a little the more), the moment I was alone I threw myself into the most violent fit of despair, and would willingly have parted with wisdom, fortune, and everything else, to have retrieved her; but that was impossible, and I had now nothing but time to hope a cure from. This was very tedious in performing it, and the longer as Ariadne had married a Roman cavalier, was now become my near neighbor, and I had the mortification of seeing her make the best of wives, and of having the happiness which I had lost, every day before my eyes.

"If I suffered so much on account of my wisdom in having refused Ariadne, I was not much more obliged to it for procuring me a rich widow, who was recommended to me by an old friend as a very prudent match; and, indeed, so it was, her fortune being superior to mine in the same proportion as that of Ariadne had been inferior. I therefore embraced this proposal, and my character of wisdom soon pleaded so effectually for me with the widow, who was herself a woman of great gravity and discretion, that I soon succeeded; and as soon as decency would permit (of which this lady was the strictest observer) we were married, being the second day of the second week of the second year after her husband's death; for she said she thought some period of time above the year had a great air of decorum.

"But, prudent as this lady was, she made me miserable. Her person was far from being lovely, but her temper was intolerable.

"During fifteen years' habitation, I never passed a single day without heartily cursing her, and the hour in which we came together. The only comfort I received, in the midst of the highest torments, was from continually hearing the prudence of my match commended by all my acquaintance.

"Thus you see, in the affairs of love, I bought the reputation of wisdom pretty dear. In other matters I had it somewhat cheaper; not that hypocrisy, which was the price I gave for it, gives one no pain. I have refused myself a thousand little amusements with a feigned contempt, while I have really had an inclination to them. I have often almost choked myself to restrain from laughing at a jest, and (which was perhaps to myself the least hurtful of all my hypocrisy) have heartily enjoyed a book in my closet which I have spoken with detestation of in public. To sum up my history in short, as I had few adventures worth remembering, my whole life was one constant lie; and happy would it have been for me if I could as thoroughly have imposed on myself as I did on others: for reflection, at every turn, would often remind me I was not so wise as people thought me; and this considerably embittered the pleasure I received from the public commendation of my wisdom. This self-admonition, like a memento mori or mortalis es, must be, in my opinion, a very dangerous enemy to flattery: indeed, a weight sufficient to counterbalance all the false praise of the world. But whether it be that the generality of wise men do not reflect at all, or whether they have, from a constant imposition on others, contracted such a habit of deceit as to deceive themselves, I will not determine: it is, I believe, most certain that very few wise men know themselves what fools they are, more than the world doth. Good gods! could one but see what passes in the closet of wisdom! how ridiculous a sight must it be to behold the wise man, who despises gratifying his palate, devouring custard; the sober wise man with his dram-bottle; or, the anti-carnalist (if I may be allowed the expression) chuckling over a b--dy book or picture, and perhaps caressing his house-maid!

"But to conclude a character in which I apprehend I made as absurd a figure as in any in which I trod the stage of earth, my wisdom at last but an end to itself, that is, occasioned my dissolution.

"A relation of mine in the eastern part of the empire disinherited his son, and left me his heir. This happened in the depth of winter, when I was in my grand climacteric, and had just recovered of a dangerous disease. As I had all the reason imaginable to apprehend the family of the deceased would conspire against me, and embezzle as much as they could, I advised with a grave and wise friend what was proper to be done; whether I should go myself, or employ a notary on this occasion, and defer my journey to the spring. To say the truth, I was most inclined to the latter; the rather as my circumstances were extremely flourishing, as I was advanced in years, and had not one person in the world to whom I should with pleasure bequeath any fortune at my death.

"My friend told me he thought my question admitted of no manner of doubt or debate; that common prudence absolutely required my immediate departure; adding, that if the same good luck had happened to him he would have been already on his journey; 'for,' continued he, 'a man who knows the world so well as you, would be inexcusable to give persons such an opportunity of cheating you, who, you must be assured, will be too well inclined; and as for employing a notary, remember that excellent maxim, Ne facias per alium, quod fieri potest per te. I own the badness of the season and your very late recovery are unlucky circumstances; but a wise man must get over difficulties when necessity obliges him to encounter them.'

"I was immediately determined by this opinion. The duty of a wise man made an irresistible impression, and I took the necessity for granted without examination. I accordingly set forward the next morning; very tempestuous weather soon overtook me; I had not traveled three days before I relapsed into my fever, and died.

"I was now as cruelly disappointed by Minos as I had formerly been happily so. I advanced with the utmost confidence to the gate, and really imagined I should have been admitted by the wisdom of my countenance, even without any questions asked: but this was not my case; and, to my great surprise, Minos, with a menacing voice, called out to me, 'You Mr. there, with the grave countenance, whither so fast, pray? Will you please, before you move any farther forwards, to give me a short account of your transactions below?' I then began, and recounted to him my whole history, still expecting at the end of every period that the gate would be ordered to fly open; but I was obliged to go quite through with it, and then Minos after some little consideration spoke to me as follows:

"'You, Mr. Wiseman, stand forth if you please. Believe me, sir, a trip back again to earth will be one of the wisest steps you ever took, and really more to the honor of your wisdom than any you have hitherto taken. On the other side, nothing could be simpler than to endeavor at Elysium; for who but a fool would carry a commodity, which is of such infinite value in one place, into another where it is of none? But, without attempting to offend your gravity with a jest, you must return to the place from whence you came, for Elysium was never designed for those who are too wise to be happy.'

"This sentence confounded me greatly, especially as it seemed to threaten me with carrying my wisdom back again to earth. I told the judge, though he would not admit me at the gate, I hoped I had committed no crime while alive which merited my being wise any longer. He answered me, I must take my chance as to that matter, and immediately we turned our backs to each other."

CHAPTER XVII

Julian enters into the person of a king.

"I was now born at Oviedo in Spain. My father's name was Veremond, and I was adopted by my uncle king Alphonso the chaste.

"I don't recollect in all the pilgrimages I have made on earth that I ever passed a more miserable infancy than now; being under the utmost confinement and restraint, and surrounded with physicians who were ever dosing me, and tutors who were continually plaguing me with their instructions; even those hours of leisure which my inclination would have spent in play were allotted to tedious pomp and ceremony, which, at an age wherein I had no ambition to enjoy the servility of courtiers, enslaved me more than it could the meanest of them. However, as I advanced towards manhood, my condition made me some amends; for the most beautiful women of their own accord threw out lures for me, and I had the happiness, which no man in an inferior degree can arrive at, of enjoying the most delicious creatures, without the previous and tiresome ceremonies of courtship, unless with the most simple, young and unexperienced. As for the court ladies, they regarded me rather as men do the most lovely of the other sex; and, though they outwardly retained some appearance of modesty, they in reality rather considered themselves as receiving than conferring favors.

"Another happiness I enjoyed was in conferring favors of another sort; for, as I was extremely good-natured and generous, so I had daily opportunities of satisfying those passions. Besides my own princely allowance, which was very bountiful, and with which I did many liberal and good actions, I recommended numberless persons of merit in distress to the king's notice, most of whom were provided for. Indeed, had I sufficiently known my blessed situation at this time, I should have grieved at nothing more than the death of Alphonso, by which the burden of government devolved upon me; but, so blindly fond is ambition, and such charms doth it fancy in the power and pomp and splendor of a crown, that, though I vehemently loved that king, and had the greatest obligations to him, the thoughts of succeeding him obliterated my regret at his loss, and the wish for my approaching coronation dried my eyes at his funeral.

"But my fondness for the name of king did not make me forgetful of those over whom I was to reign. I considered them in the light in which a tender father regards his children, as persons whose wellbeing God had intrusted to my care; and again, in that in which a prudent lord respects his tenants, as those on whose wealth and grandeur he is to build his own. Both these considerations inspired me with the greatest care for their welfare, and their good was my first and ultimate concern.

"The usurper Mauregas had impiously obliged himself and his successors to pay to the Moors every year an infamous tribute of an hundred young virgins: from this cruel and scandalous imposition I resolved to relieve my country. Accordingly, when their emperor Abderames the second had the audaciousness to make this demand of me, instead of complying with it I ordered his ambassadors to be driven away with all imaginable ignominy, and would have condemned them to death, could I have done it without a manifest violation of the law of nations.

"I now raised an immense army; at the levying of which I made a speech from my throne, acquainting my subjects with the necessity and the reasons of the war in which I was going to engage: which I convinced them I had undertaken for their ease and safety, and not for satisfying any wanton ambition, or revenging any private pique of my own. They all declared unanimously that they would venture their lives and everything dear to them in my defense, and in the support of the honor of my crown. Accordingly, my levies were instantly complete, sufficient numbers being only left to till the land; churchmen, even bishops themselves, enlisting themselves under my banners.

"The armies met at Alvelda, where we were discomfited with immense loss, and nothing but the lucky intervention of the night could have saved our whole army.

"I retreated to the summit of a hill, where I abandoned myself to the highest agonies of grief, not so much for the danger in which I then saw my crown, as for the loss of those miserable wretches who had exposed their lives at my command. I could not then avoid this reflection, that, if the deaths of these people in a war undertaken absolutely for their protection could give me such concern, what horror must I have felt if, like princes greedy of dominion, I had sacrificed such numbers to my own pride, vanity, and ridiculous lust of power.

"After having vented my sorrows for some time in this manner, I began to consider by what means I might possibly endeavor to retrieve this misfortune; when, reflecting on the great number of priests I had in my army, and on the prodigious force of superstition, a thought luckily suggested itself to me, to counterfeit that St. James had appeared to me in a vision, and had promised me the victory. While I was ruminating on this the bishop of Najara came opportunely to me. As I did not intend to communicate the secret to him, I took another method, and, instead of answering anything the bishop said to me, I pretended to talk to St. James, as if he had been really present; till at length, after having spoke those things which I thought sufficient, and thanked the saint aloud for his promise of the victory, I turned about to the bishop, and, embracing him with a pleased countenance, protested I did not know he was present; and then, informing him of this supposed vision, I asked him if he had not himself seen the saint? He answered me he had; and afterwards proceeded to assure me that this appearance of St. James was entirely owing to his prayers; for that he was his tutelar saint. He added he had a vision of him a few hours before, when he promised him a victory over the infidels, and acquainted him at the same time of the vacancy of the see of Toledo. Now, this news being really true, though it had happened so lately that I had not heard of it (nor, indeed, was it well possible I should, considering the great distance of the way), when I was afterwards acquainted with it, a little staggered me, though far from being superstitious; till being informed that the bishop had lost three horses on a late expedition, I was satisfied.

"The next morning, the bishop, at my desire, mounted the rostrum, and trumpeted forth this vision so effectually, which he said he had that evening twice seen with his own eyes, that a spirit began to be infused through the whole army which rendered them superior to almost any force: the bishop insisted that the least doubt of success was giving the lie to the saint, and a damnable sin, and he took upon him in his name to promise them victory.

"The army being drawn out, I soon experienced the effect of enthusiasm, for, having contrived another stratagem [9] to strengthen what the bishop had said, the soldiers fought more like furies than men. My stratagem was this: I had about me a dexterous fellow, who had been formerly a pimp in my amours. Him I dressed up in a strange antic dress, with a pair of white colors in his right hand, a red cross in his left, and having disguised him so that no one could know him, I placed him on a white horse, and ordered him to ride to the head of the army, and cry out, 'Follow St. James!' These words were reiterated by all the troops, who attacked the enemy with such intrepidity, that, notwithstanding our inferiority of numbers, we soon obtained a complete victory.

"The bishop was come up by the time that the enemy was routed, and, acquainting us that he had met St. James by the way, and that he had informed him of what had passed, he added that he had express orders from the saint to receive a considerable sum for his use, and that a certain tax on corn and wine should be settled on his church for ever; and lastly, that a horseman's pay should be allowed for the future to the saint himself, of which he and his successors were appointed receivers. The army received these demands with such acclamations that I was obliged to comply with them, as I could by no means discover the imposition, nor do I believe I should have gained any credit if I had.

"I had now done with the saint, but the bishop had not; for about a week afterwards lights were seen in a wood near where the battle was fought; and in a short time afterwards they discovered his tomb at the same place. Upon this the bishop made me a visit, and forced me to go thither, to build a church to him, and largely endow it. In a word, the good man so plagued me with miracle after miracle, that I was forced to make interest with the pope to convey him to Toledo, to get rid of him.

"But to proceed to other matters. There was an inferior officer, who had behaved very bravely in the battle against the Moors, and had received several wounds, who solicited me for preferment; which I was about to confer on him, when one of my ministers came to me in a fright, and told me that he had promised the post I designed for this man to the son of count Alderedo; and that the count, who was a powerful person, would be greatly disobliged at the refusal, as he had sent for his son from school to take possession of it. I was obliged to agree with my minister's reasons, and at the same time recommended the wounded soldier to be preferred by him, which he faithfully promised he would; but I met the poor wretch since in Elysium, who informed me he was afterwards starved to death.

"None who hath not been himself a prince, nor any prince till his death, can conceive the impositions daily put on them by their favorites and ministers; so that princes are often blamed for the faults of others. The count of Saldagne had been long confined in prison, when his son, D. Bernard del Carpio, who had performed the greatest actions against the Moors, entreated me, as a reward for his service, to grant him his father's liberty. The old man's punishment had been so tedious, and the services of the young one so singularly eminent, that I was very inclinable to grant the request; but my ministers strongly opposed it; they told me my glory demanded revenge for the dishonor offered to my family; that so positive a demand carried with it rather the air of menace than entreaty; that the vain detail of his services, and the recompense due to them, was an injurious reproach; that to grant what had been so haughtily demanded would argue in the monarch both weakness and timidity; in a word, that to remit the punishment inflicted by my predecessors would be to condemn their judgment. Lastly, one told me in a whisper, 'His whole family are enemies to your house.' By these means the ministers prevailed. The young lord took the refusal so ill, that he retired from court, and abandoned himself to despair, whilst the old one languished in prison. By which means, as I have since discovered, I lost the use of two of my best subjects.

"To confess the truth, I had, by means of my ministers, conceived a very unjust opinion of my whole people, whom I fancied to be daily conspiring against me, and to entertain the most disloyal thoughts, when, in reality (as I have known since my death), they held me in universal respect and esteem. This is a trick, I believe, too often played with sovereigns, who, by such means, are prevented from that open intercourse with their subjects which, as it would greatly endear the person of the prince to the people, so might it often prove dangerous to a minister who was consulting his own interest only at the expense of both. I believe I have now recounted to you the most material passages of my life; for I assure you there are some incidents in the lives of kings not extremely worth relating. Everything which passes in their minds and families is not attended with the splendor which surrounds their throne, indeed, there are some hours wherein the naked king and the naked cobbler can scarce be distinguished from each other.

"Had it not been, however, for my ingratitude to Bernard del Carpio, I believe this would have been my last pilgrimage on earth; for, as to the story of St. James, I thought Minos would have burst his sides at it; but he was so displeased with me on the other account, that, with a frown, he cried out, 'Get thee back again, king.' Nor would he suffer me to say another word."

CHAPTER XVIII

Julian passes into a fool.

"The next visit I made to the world was performed in France, where I was born in the court of Lewis III, and had afterwards the honor to be preferred to be fool to the prince, who was surnamed Charles the Simple. But, in reality, I know not whether I might so properly be said to have acted the fool in his court as to have made fools of all others in it. Certain it is, I was very far from being what is generally understood by that word, being a most cunning, designing, arch knave. I knew very well the folly of my master, and of many others, and how to make my advantage of this knowledge.

"I was as dear to Charles the Simple as the player Paris was to Domitian, and, like him, bestowed all manner of offices and honors on whom I pleased. This drew me a great number of followers among the courtiers, who really mistook me for a fool, and yet flattered my understanding. There was particularly in the court a fellow who had neither honor, honesty, sense, wit, courage, beauty, nor indeed any one good quality, either of mind or body, to recommend him; but was at the same time, perhaps, as cunning a monster as ever lived. This gentleman took it into his head to list under my banner, and pursued me so very assiduously with flattery, constantly reminding me of my good sense, that I grew immoderately fond of him; for though flattery is not most judiciously applied to qualities which the persons flattered possess, yet as, notwithstanding my being well assured of my own parts, I passed in the whole court for a fool, this flattery was a very sweet morsel to me. I therefore got this fellow preferred to a bishopric, but I lost my flatterer by it; for he never afterwards said a civil thing to me.

"I never balked my imagination for the grossness of the reflection on the character of the greatest noble, nay, even the king himself; of which I will give you a very bold instance. One day his simple majesty told me he believed I had so much power that his people looked on me as the king, and himself as my fool.

"At this I pretended to be angry, as with an affront. 'Why, how now?' says the king; 'are you ashamed of being a king?' 'No, sir,' says I, 'but I am devilishly ashamed of my fool.'

"Herbert, earl of Vermandois, had by my means been restored to the favor of the Simple (for so I used always to call Charles). He afterwards prevailed with the king to take the city of Arras from earl Baldwin, by which means, Herbert, in exchange for this city, had Peronne restored to him by count Altmar. Baldwin came to court in order to procure the restoration of his city; but, either through pride or ignorance, neglected to apply to me. As I met him at court during his solicitation, I told him he did not apply the right way; he answered roughly he should not ask a fool's advice. I replied I did not wonder at his prejudice, since he had miscarried already by following a fool's advice; but I told him there were fools who had more interest than that he had brought with him to court. He answered me surlily he had no fool with him, for that he traveled alone. 'Ay, my lord,' says I, 'I often travel alone, and yet they will have it I always carry a fool with me.' This raised a laugh among the by-standers, on which he gave me a blow. I immediately complained of this usage to the Simple, who dismissed the earl from court with very hard words, instead of granting him the favor he solicited.

"I give you these rather as a specimen of my interest and impudence than of my wit, indeed, my jests were commonly more admired than they ought to be; for perhaps I was not in reality much more a wit than a fool. But, with the latitude of unbounded scurrility, it is easy enough to attain the character of wit, especially in a court, where, as all persons hate and envy one another heartily, and are at the same time obliged by the constrained behavior of civility to profess the greatest liking, so it is, and must be, wonderfully pleasant to them to see the follies of their acquaintance exposed by a third person. Besides, the opinion of the court is as uniform as the fashion, and is always guided by the will of the prince or of the favorite. I doubt not that Caligula's horse was universally held in his court to be a good and able consul. In the same manner was I universally acknowledged to be the wittiest fool in the world. Every word I said raised laughter, and was held to be a jest, especially by the ladies, who sometimes laughed before I had discovered my sentiment, and often repeated that as a jest which I did not even intend as one.

"I was as severe on the ladies as on the men, and with the same impunity; but this at last cost me dear: for once having joked on the beauty of a lady whose name was Adelaide, a favorite of the Simple's, she pretended to smile and be pleased at my wit with the rest of the company; but in reality she highly resented it, and endeavored to undermine me with the king. In which she so greatly succeeded (for what cannot a favorite woman do with one who deserves the surname of Simple?) that the king grew every day more reserved to me, and when I attempted any freedom gave me such marks of his displeasure, that the courtiers who have all hawks' eyes at a slight from the sovereign, soon discerned it: and indeed, had I been blind enough not to have discovered that I had lost ground in the Simple's favor by his own change in his carriage towards me, I must have found it, nay even felt it, in the behavior of the courtiers: for, as my company was two days before solicited with the utmost eagerness, it was now rejected with as much scorn. I was now the jest of the ushers and pages; and an officer of the guards, on whom I was a little jocose, gave me a box on the ear, bidding me make free with my equals. This very fellow had been my butt for many years, without daring to lift his hand against me.

"But though I visibly perceived the alteration in the Simple, I was utterly unable to make any guess at the occasion. I had not the least suspicion of Adelaide; for, besides her being a very good-humored woman, I had often made severe jests on her reputation, which I had all the reason imaginable to believe had given her no offense. But I soon perceived that a woman will bear the most bitter censures on her morals easier than the smallest reflection on her beauty; for she now declared publicly, that I ought to be dismissed from court, as the stupidest of fools, and one in whom there was no diversion; and that she wondered how any person could have so little taste as to imagine I had any wit. This speech was echoed through the drawing-room, and agreed to by all present. Every one now put on an unusual gravity on their countenance whenever I spoke; and it was as much out of my power to raise a laugh as formerly it had been for me to open my mouth without one.

"While my affairs were in this posture I went one day into the circle without my fool's dress. The Simple, who would still speak to me, cried out, 'So, fool, what's the matter now?' 'Sir,' answered I, 'fools are like to be so common a commodity at court, that I am weary of my coat.' 'How dost thou mean?' answered the Simple; 'what can make them commoner now than usual?' - 'O, sir,' said I, 'there are ladies here make your majesty a fool every day of their lives.' The Simple took no notice of my jest, and several present said my bones ought to be broke for my impudence; but it pleased the queen, who, knowing Adelaide, whom she hated, to be the cause of my disgrace, obtained me of the king, and took me into her service; so that I was henceforth called the queen's fool, and in her court received the same honor, and had as much wit, as I had formerly had in the king's. But as the queen had really no power unless over her own domestics, I was not treated in general with that complacence, nor did I receive those bribes and presents, which had once fallen to my share.

"Nor did this confined respect continue long: for the queen, who had in fact no taste for humor, soon grew sick of my foolery, and, forgetting the cause for which she had taken me, neglected me so much, that her court grew intolerable to my temper, and I broke my heart and died.

"Minos laughed heartily at several things in my story, and then, telling me no one played the fool in Elysium, bid me go back again."

CHAPTER XIX

Julian appears in the character of a beggar.

"I now returned to Rome, and was born into a very poor and numerous family, which, to be honest with you, procured its livelihood by begging. This, if you was never yourself of the calling, you do not know, I suppose, to be as regular a trade as any other; to have its several rules and secrets, or mysteries, which to learn require perhaps as tedious an apprenticeship as those of any craft whatever.

"The first thing we are taught is the countenance miserable. This indeed nature makes much easier to some than others; but there are none who cannot accomplish it, if they begin early enough in youth, and before the muscles are grown too stubborn.

"The second thing is the voice lamentable. In this qualification too, nature must have her share in producing the most consummate excellence: however, art will here, as in every other instance, go a great way with industry and application, even without the assistance of genius, especially if the student begins young.

"There are many other instructions, but these are the most considerable. The women are taught one practice more than the men, for they are instructed in the art of crying, that is, to have their tears ready on all occasions: but this is attained very easily by most. Some indeed arrive at the utmost perfection in this art with incredible facility.

"No profession requires a deeper insight into human nature than the beggar's. Their knowledge of the passions of men is so extensive, that I have often thought it would be of no little service to a politician to have his education among them. Nay, there is a much greater analogy between these two characters than is imagined; for both concur in their first and grand principle, it being equally their business to delude and impose on mankind. It must be confessed that they differ widely in the degree of advantage which they make by their deceit; for, whereas the beggar is contented with a little, the politician leaves but a little behind.

"A very great English philosopher hath remarked our policy, in taking care never to address any one with a title inferior to what he really claims. My father was of the same opinion; for I remember when I was a boy, the pope happening to pass by, I tended him with 'Pray, sir;' 'For God's sake, sir;' 'For the Lord's sake, sir;' To which he answered gravely, 'Sirrah, sirrah, you ought to be whipped for taking the Lord's name in vain;' and in vain it was indeed, for he gave me nothing. My father, overhearing this, took his advice, and whipped me very severely. While I was under correction I promised often never to take the Lord's name in vain any more. My father then said, 'Child, I do not whip you for taking his name in vain; I whip you for not calling the pope his holiness.'

"If all men were so wise and good to follow the clergy's example, the nuisance of beggars would soon be removed. I do not remember to have been above twice relieved by them during my whole state of beggary. Once was by a very well-looking man, who gave me a small piece of silver, and declared he had given me more than he had left himself; the other was by a spruce young fellow, who had that very day first put on his robes, whom I attended with 'Pray, reverend sir, good reverend sir, consider your cloth.' He answered, 'I do, child, consider my office, and I hope all our cloth do the same.' He then threw down some money, and strutted off with great dignity.

"With the women I had one general formulary: 'Sweet pretty lady,' 'God bless your ladyship,' 'God bless your handsome face.' This generally succeeded; but I observed the uglier the woman was, the surer I was of success.

"It was a constant maxim among us, that the greater retinue any one traveled with the less expectation we might promise ourselves from them; but whenever we saw a vehicle with a single or no servant we imagined our booty sure, and were seldom deceived.

"We observed great difference introduced by time and circumstance in the same person; for instance, a losing gamester is sometimes generous, but from a winner you will as easily obtain his soul as a single groat. A lawyer traveling from his country seat to his clients at Rome, and a physician going to visit a patient, were always worth asking; but the same on their return were (according to our cant phrase) untouchable.

"The most general, and indeed the truest, maxim among us was, that those who possessed the least were always the readiest to give. The chief art of a beggar-man is, therefore, to discern the rich from the poor, which, though it be only distinguishing substance from shadow, is by no means attainable without a pretty good capacity and a vast degree of attention; for these two are eternally industrious in endeavoring to counterfeit each other. In this deceit the poor man is more heartily in earnest to deceive you than the rich, who, amidst all the emblems of poverty which he puts on, still permits some mark of his wealth to strike the eye. Thus, while his apparel is not worth a groat, his finger wears a ring of value, or his pocket a gold watch. In a word, he seems rather to affect poverty to insult than impose on you. Now the poor man, on the contrary, is very sincere in his desire of passing for rich; but the eagerness of this desire hurries him to over-act his part, and he betrays himself as one who is drunk by his overacted sobriety. Thus, instead of being attended by one servant well mounted, he will have two; and, not being able to purchase or maintain a second horse of value, one of his servants at least is mounted on a hired rascallion. He is not contented to go plain and neat in his clothes; he therefore claps on some tawdry ornament, and what he adds to the fineness of his vestment he detracts from the fineness of his linen. Without descending into more minute particulars, I believe I may assert it as an axiom of indubitable truth, that whoever shows you he is either in himself or his equipage as gaudy as he can, convinces you he is more so than he can afford. Now, whenever a man's expense exceeds his income, he is indifferent in the degree; we had therefore nothing more to do with such than to flatter them with their wealth and splendor, and were always certain of success.

"There is, indeed, one kind of rich man who is commonly more liberal, namely, where riches surprise him, as it were, in the midst of poverty and distress, the consequence of which is, I own, sometimes excessive avarice, but oftener extreme prodigality. I remember one of these who, having received a pretty large sum of money, gave me, when I begged an obolus, a whole talent; on which his friend having reproved him, he answered, with an oath, 'Why not? Have I not fifty left?'

"The life of a beggar, if men estimated things by their real essence, and not by their outward false appearance, would be, perhaps, a more desirable situation than any of those which ambition persuades us, with such difficulty, danger, and often villainy, to aspire to. The wants of a beggar are commonly as chimerical as the abundance of a nobleman; for besides vanity, which a judicious beggar will always apply to with wonderful efficacy, there are in reality very few natures so hardened as not to compassionate poverty and distress, when the predominancy of some other passion doth not prevent them.

"There is one happiness which attends money got with ease, namely, that it is never hoarded; otherwise, as we have frequent opportunities of growing rich, that canker care might prey upon our quiet, as it doth on others; but our money stock we spend as fast as we acquire it; usually at least, for I speak not without exception; thus it gives us mirth only, and no trouble. Indeed, the luxury of our lives might introduce diseases, did not our daily exercise prevent them. This gives us an appetite and relish for our dainties, and at the same time an antidote against the evil effects which sloth, united with luxury, induces on the habit of a human body. Our women we enjoy with ecstasies at least equal to what the greatest men feel in their embraces. I can, I am assured, say of myself, that no mortal could reap more perfect happiness from the tender passion than my fortune had decreed me. I married a charming young woman for love; she was the daughter of a neighboring beggar, who, with an improvidence too often seen, spent a very large income which he procured by his profession, so that he was able to give her no fortune down; however, at his death he left her a very well accustomed begging-hut, situated on the side of a steep hill, where travelers could not immediately escape from us, and a garden adjoining, being the twenty-eighth part of an acre, well planted.

"She made the best of wives, bore me nineteen children, and never failed, unless on her lying-in, which generally lasted three days, to get my supper ready against my return home in an evening; this being my favorite meal, and at which I, as well as my whole family, greatly enjoyed ourselves; the principal subject of our discourse being generally the boons we had that day obtained, on which occasions, laughing at the folly of the donors made no inconsiderable part of the entertainment; for, whatever might be their motive for giving, we constantly imputed our success to our having flattered their vanity, or overreached their understanding.

"But perhaps I have dwelt too long on this character; I shall conclude, therefore, with telling you that after a life of 102 years' continuance, during all which I had never known any sickness or infirmity but that which old age necessarily induced, I at last, without the least pain, went out like the snuff of a candle.

"Minos, having heard my history, bid me compute, if I could, how many lies I had told in my life. As we are here, by a certain fated necessity, obliged to confine ourselves to truth, I answered, I believed about 50,000,000. He then replied, with a frown, 'Can such a wretch conceive any hopes of entering Elysium?' I immediately turned about, and, upon the whole, was rejoiced at his not calling me back."

CHAPTER XX

Julian performs the part of a statesman.

"It was now my fortune to be born of a German princess; but a man-midwife, pulling my head off in delivering my mother, put a speedy end to my princely life.

"Spirits who end their lives before they are at the age of five years are immediately ordered into other bodies; and it was now my fortune to perform several infancies before I could again entitle myself to an examination of Minos.

"At length I was destined once more to play a considerable part on the stage. I was born in England, in the reign of Ethelred II. My father's name was Ulnoth: he was earl or thane of Sussex. I was afterwards known by the name of earl Goodwin, and began to make a considerable figure in the world in the time of Harold Harefoot, whom I procured to be made king of Wessex, or the West Saxons, in prejudice of Hardicanute, whose mother Emma endeavored afterwards to set another of her sons on the throne; but I circumvented her, and, communicating her design to the king, at the same time acquainted him with a project which I had formed for the murder of these two young princes. Emma had sent for these her sons from Normandy, with the king's leave, whom she had deceived by her religious behavior, and pretended neglect of all worldly affairs; but I prevailed with Harold to invite these princes to his court, and put them to death. The prudent mother sent only Alfred, retaining Edward to herself, as she suspected my ill designs, and thought I should not venture to execute them on one of her sons, while she secured the other; but she was deceived, for I had no sooner Alfred in my possession than I caused him to be conducted to Ely, where I ordered his eyes to be put out, and afterwards to be confined in a monastery.

"This was one of those cruel expedients which great men satisfy themselves well in executing, by concluding them to be necessary to the service of their prince, who is the support of their ambition.

"Edward, the other son of Emma, escaped again to Normandy; whence, after the death of Harold and Hardicanute, he made no scruple of applying to my protection and favor, though he had before prosecuted me with all the vengeance he was able, for the murder of his brother; but in all great affairs private relation must yield to public interest. Having therefore concluded very advantageous terms for myself with him, I made no scruple of patronizing his cause, and soon placed him on the throne. Nor did I conceive the least apprehension from his resentment, as I knew my power was too great for him to encounter.

"Among other stipulated conditions, one was to marry my daughter Editha. This Edward consented to with great reluctance, and I had afterwards no reason to be pleased with it; for it raised her, who had been my favorite child, to such an opinion of greatness, that, instead of paying me the usual respect, she frequently threw in my teeth (as often at least as I gave her any admonition), that she was now a queen, and that the character and title of father merged in that of subject. This behavior, however, did not cure me of my affection towards her, nor lessen the uneasiness which I afterwards bore on Edward's dismissing her from his bed.

"One thing which principally induced me to labor the promotion of Edward was the simplicity or weakness of that prince, under whom I promised myself absolute dominion under another name. Nor did this opinion deceive me; for, during his whole reign, my administration was in the highest degree despotic: I had everything of royalty but the outward ensigns; no man ever applying for a place, or any kind of preferment, but to me only. A circumstance which, as it greatly enriched my coffers, so it no less pampered my ambition, and satisfied my vanity with a numerous attendance; and I had the pleasure of seeing those who only bowed to the king prostrating themselves before me.

"Edward the Confessor, or St. Edward, as some have called him, in derision I suppose, being a very silly fellow, had all the faults incident, and almost inseparable, to fools. He married my daughter Editha from his fear of disobliging me; and afterwards, out of hatred to me, refused even to consummate his marriage, though she was one of the most beautiful women of her age. He was likewise guilty of the basest ingratitude to his mother (a vice to which fools are chiefly, if not only, liable); and, in return for her endeavors to procure him a throne in his youth, confined her in a loathsome prison in her old age. This, it is true, he did by my advice; but as to her walking over nine plowshares red-hot, and giving nine manors, when she had not one in her possession, there is not a syllable of veracity in it.

"The first great perplexity I fell into was on the account of my son Swane, who had deflowered the abbess of Leon, since called Leominster, in Herefordshire. After this fact he retired into Denmark, whence he sent to me to obtain his pardon. The king at first refused it, being moved thereto, as I afterwards found, by some churchmen, particularly by one of his chaplains, whom I had prevented from obtaining a bishopric. Upon this my son Swane invaded the coasts with several ships, and committed many outrageous cruelties; which, indeed, did his business, as they served me to apply to the fear of this king, which I had long since discovered to be his predominant passion. And, at last, he who had refused pardon to his first offense submitted to give it him after he had committed many other more monstrous crimes; by which his pardon lost all grace to the offended, and received double censure from all others.

"The king was greatly inclined to the Normans, had created a Norman archbishop of Canterbury, and had heaped extraordinary favors on him. I had no other objection to this man than that he rose without my assistance; a cause of dislike which, in the reign of great and powerful favorites, hath often proved fatal to the persons who have given it, as the persons thus raised inspire us constantly with jealousies and apprehensions. For when we promote any one ourselves, we take effectual care to preserve such an ascendant over him, that we can at any time reduce him to his former degree, should he dare to act in opposition to our wills; for which reason we never suffer any to come near the prince but such as we are assured it is impossible should be capable of engaging or improving his affection; no prime minister, as I apprehend, esteeming himself to be safe while any other shares the ear of his prince, of whom we are as jealous as the fondest husband can be of his wife. Whoever, therefore, can approach him by any other channel than that of ourselves, is, in our opinion, a declared enemy, and one whom the first principles of policy oblige us to demolish with the utmost expedition. For the affection of kings is as precarious as that of women, and the only way to secure either to ourselves is to keep all others from them.

"But the archbishop did not let matters rest on suspicion. He soon gave open proofs of his interest with the Confessor in procuring an office of some importance for one Rollo, a Roman of mean extraction and very despicable parts. When I represented to the king the indecency of conferring such an honor on such a fellow, he answered me that he was the archbishop's relation. 'Then, sir,' replied I, 'he is related to your enemy.' Nothing more passed at that time; but I soon perceived, by the archbishop's behavior, that the king had acquainted him with our private discourse; a sufficient assurance of his confidence in him and neglect of me.

"The favor of princes, when once lost, is recoverable only by the gaining a situation which may make you terrible to them. As I had no doubt of having lost all credit with this king, which indeed had been originally founded and constantly supported by his fear, so I took the method of terror to regain it.

"The earl of Boulogne coming over to visit the king gave me an opportunity of breaking out into open opposition; for, as the earl was on his return to France, one of his servants, who was sent before to procure lodgings at Dover, and insisted on having them in the house of a private man in spite of the owner's teeth, was, in a fray which ensued, killed on the spot; and the earl himself, arriving there soon after, very narrowly escaped with his life. The earl, enraged at this affront, returned to the king at Gloucester with loud complaints and demands of satisfaction. Edward consented to his demands, and ordered me to chastise the rioters, who were under my government as earl of Kent: but, instead of obeying these orders, I answered, with some warmth, that the English were not used to punish people unheard, nor ought their rights and privileges to be violated; that the accused should be first summoned, if guilty, should make satisfaction both with body and estate, but, if innocent, should be discharged. Adding, with great ferocity, that as earl of Kent it was my duty to protect those under my government against the insults of foreigners.

"This accident was extremely lucky, as it gave my quarrel with the king a popular color, and so ingratiated me with the people, that when I set up my standard, which I soon after did, they readily and cheerfully listed under my banners and embraced my cause, which I persuaded them was their own; for that it was to protect them against foreigners that I had drawn my sword. The word foreigners with an Englishman hath a kind of magical effect, they having the utmost hatred and aversion to them, arising from the cruelties they suffered from the Danes and some other foreign nations. No wonder therefore they espoused my cause in a quarrel which had such a beginning.

"But what may be somewhat more remarkable is, that when I afterwards returned to England from banishment, and was at the head of an army of the Flemish, who were preparing to plunder the city of London, I still persisted that I was come to defend the English from the danger of foreigners, and gained their credit. Indeed, there is no lie so gross but it may be imposed on the people by those whom they esteem their patrons and defenders.

"The king saved his city by being reconciled to me, and taking again my daughter, whom he had put away from him; and thus, having frightened the king into what concessions I thought proper, I dismissed my army and fleet, with which I intended, could I not have succeeded otherwise, to have sacked the city of London and ravaged the whole country.

"I was no sooner re-established in the king's favor, or, what was as well for me, the appearance of it, than I fell violently on the archbishop. He had of himself retired to his monastery in Normandy; but that did not content me: I had him formally banished, the see declared vacant, and then filled up by another.

"I enjoyed my grandeur a very short time after my restoration to it; for the king, hating and fearing me to a very great degree, and finding no means of openly destroying me, at last effected his purpose by poison, and then spread abroad a ridiculous story, of my wishing the next morsel might choke me if I had had any hand in the death of Alfred; and, accordingly, that the next morsel, by a divine judgment, stuck in my throat and performed that office.

"This of a statesman was one of my worst stages in the other world. It is a post subjected daily to the greatest danger and inquietude, and attended with little pleasure and less ease. In a word, it is a pill which, was it not gilded over by ambition, would appear nauseous and detestable in the eye of every one; and perhaps that is one reason why Minos so greatly compassionates the case of those who swallow it: for that just judge told me he always acquitted a prime minister who could produce one single good action in his whole life, let him have committed ever so many crimes. Indeed, I understood him a little too largely, and was stepping towards the gate; but he pulled me by the sleeve, and, telling me no prime minister ever entered there, bid me go back again; saying, he thought I had sufficient reason to rejoice in my escaping the bottomless pit, which half my crimes committed in any other capacity would have entitled me to."

CHAPTER XXI

Julian's adventures in the post of a soldier.

"I was born at Caen, in Normandy. My mother's name was Matilda; as for my father, I am not so certain, for the good woman on her death-bed assured me she herself could bring her guess to no greater certainty than to five of duke William's captains. When I was no more than thirteen (being indeed a surprising stout boy of my age) I enlisted into the army of duke William, afterwards known by the name of William the Conqueror, landed with him at Pemesey or Pemsey, in Sussex, and was present at the famous battle of Hastings.

"At the first onset it was impossible to describe my consternation, which was heightened by the fall of two soldiers who stood by me; but this soon abated, and by degrees, as my blood grew warm, I thought no more of my own safety, but fell on the enemy with great fury, and did a good deal of execution; till, unhappily, I received a wound in my thigh, which rendered me unable to stand any longer, so that I now lay among the dead, and was constantly exposed to the danger of being trampled to death, as well by my fellow-soldiers as by the enemy. However, I had the fortune to escape it, and continued the remaining part of the day and the night following on the ground.

"The next morning, the duke sending out parties to bring off the wounded, I was found almost expiring with loss of blood; notwithstanding which, as immediate care was taken to dress my wounds, youth and a robust constitution stood my friends, and I recovered after a long and tedious indisposition, and was again able to use my limbs and do my duty.

"As soon as Dover was taken I was conveyed thither with all the rest of the sick and wounded. Here I recovered of my wound; but fell afterwards into a violent flux, which, when it departed, left me so weak that it was long before I could regain my strength. And what most afflicted me was, that during my whole illness, when I languished under want as well as sickness, I had daily the mortification to see and hear the riots and excess of my fellow-soldiers, who had happily escaped safe from the battle.

"I was no sooner well than I was ordered into garrison at Dover Castle. The officers here fared very indifferently, but the private men much worse. We had great scarcity of provisions, and, what was yet more intolerable, were so closely confined for want of room (four of us being obliged to lie on the same bundle of straw), that many died, and most sickened.

"Here I had remained about four months, when one night we were alarmed with the arrival of the earl of Boulogne, who had come over privily from France, and endeavored to surprise the castle. The design proved ineffectual; for the garrison making a brisk sally, most of his men were tumbled down the precipice, and he returned with a very few back to France. In this action, however, I had the misfortune to come off with a broken arm; it was so shattered, that, besides a great deal of pain and misery which I endured in my cure, I was disabled for upwards of three months.

"Soon after my recovery I had contracted an amour with a young woman whose parents lived near the garrison, and were in much better circumstances than I had reason to expect should give their consent to the match. However, as she was extremely fond of me (as I was indeed distractedly enamored of her), they were prevailed on to comply with her desires, and the day was fixed for our marriage.

"On the evening preceding, while I was exulting with the eager expectation of the happiness I was the next day to enjoy, I received orders to march early in the morning towards Windsor, where a large army was to be formed, at the head of which the king intended to march into the west. Any person who hath ever been in love may easily imagine what I felt in my mind on receiving those orders; and what still heightened my torments was, that the commanding officer would not permit any one to go out of the garrison that evening; so that I had not even an opportunity of taking leave of my beloved.

"The morning came which was to have put me in the possession of my wishes; but, alas! the scene was now changed, and all the hopes which I had raised were now so many ghosts to haunt, and furies to torment me.

"It was now the midst of winter, and very severe weather for the season; when we were obliged to make very long and fatiguing marches, in which we suffered all the inconveniences of cold and hunger. The night in which I expected to riot in the arms of my beloved mistress I was obliged to take up with a lodging on the ground, exposed to the inclemencies of a rigid frost; nor could I obtain the least comfort of sleep, which shunned me as its enemy.

"In short, the horrors of that night are not to be described, or perhaps imagined. They made such an impression on my soul, that I was forced to be dipped three times in the river Lethe to prevent my remembering It in the characters which I afterwards performed in the flesh."

Here I interrupted Julian for the first time, and told him no such dipping had happened to me in my voyage from one world to the other: but he satisfied me by saying "that this only happened to those spirits which returned into the flesh, in order to prevent that reminiscence which Plato mentions, and which would otherwise cause great confusion in the other world."

He then proceeded as follows: "We continued a very laborious march to Exeter, which we were ordered to besiege. The town soon surrendered, and his majesty built a castle there, which he garrisoned with his Normans, and unhappily I had the misfortune to be one of the number.

"Here we were confined closer than I had been at Dover; for, as the citizens were extremely disaffected, we were never suffered to go without the walls of the castle; nor indeed could we, unless in large bodies, without the utmost danger. We were likewise kept to continual duty, nor could any solicitations prevail with the commanding officer to give me a month's absence to visit my love, from whom I had no opportunity of hearing in all my long absence.

"However, in the spring, the people being more quiet, and another officer of a gentler temper succeeding to the principal command, I obtained leave to go to Dover; but alas! what comfort did my long journey bring me? I found the parents of my darling in the utmost misery at her loss; for she had died, about a week before my arrival, of a consumption, which they imputed to her pining at my sudden departure.

"I now fell into the most violent and almost raving fit of despair. I cursed myself, the king, and the whole world, which no longer seemed to have any delight for me. I threw myself on the grave of my deceased love, and lay there without any kind of sustenance for two whole days. At last hunger, together with the persuasions of some people who took pity on me, prevailed with me to quit that situation, and refresh myself with food. They then persuaded me to return to my post, and abandon a place where almost every object I saw recalled ideas to my mind which, as they said, I should endeavor with my utmost force to expel from it. This advice at length succeeded; the rather, as the father and mother of my beloved refused to see me, looking on me as the innocent but certain cause of the death of their only child.

"The loss of one we tenderly love, as it is one of the most bitter and biting evils which attend human life, so it wants the lenitive which palliates and softens every other calamity; I mean that great reliever, hope. No man can be so totally undone, but that he may still cherish expectation: but this deprives us of all such comfort, nor can anything but time alone lessen it. This, however, in most minds, is sure to work a slow but effectual remedy; so did it in mine: for within a twelve-month I was entirely reconciled to my fortune, and soon after absolutely forgot the object of a passion from which I had promised myself such extreme happiness, and in the disappointment of which I had experienced such inconceivable misery.

"At the expiration of the month I returned to my garrison at Exeter; where I was no sooner arrived than I was ordered to march into the north, to oppose a force there levied by the earls of Chester and Northumberland. We came to York, where his majesty pardoned the heads of the rebels, and very severely punished some who were less guilty. It was particularly my lot to be ordered to seize a poor man who had never been out of his house, and convey him to prison. I detested this barbarity, yet was obliged to execute it; nay, though no reward would have bribed me in a private capacity to have acted such a part, yet so much sanctity is there in the commands of a monarch or general to a soldier, that I performed it without reluctance, nor had the tears of his wife and family any prevalence with me.

"But this, which was a very small piece of mischief in comparison with many of my barbarities afterwards, was however, the only one which ever gave me any uneasiness; for when the king led us afterwards into Northumberland to revenge those people's having joined with Osborne the Dane in his invasion, and orders were given us to commit what ravages we could, I was forward in fulfilling them, and, among some lesser cruelties (I remember it yet with sorrow), I ravished a woman, murdered a little infant playing in her lap, and then burned her house. In short, for I have no pleasure in this part of my relation, I had my share in all the cruelties exercised on those poor wretches; which were so grievous, that for sixty miles together, between York and Durham, not a single house, church, or any other public or private edifice, was left standing.

"We had pretty well devoured the country, when we were ordered to march to the Isle of Ely, to oppose Hereward, a bold and stout soldier, who had under him a very large body of rebels, who had the impudence to rise against their king and conqueror (I talk now in the same style I did then) in defense of their liberties, as they called them. These were soon subdued; but as I happened (more to my glory than my comfort) to be posted in that part through which Hereward cut his way, I received a dreadful cut on the forehead, a second on the shoulder, and was run through the body with a pike.

"I languished a long time with these wounds, which made me incapable of attending the king into Scotland. However, I was able to go over with him afterwards into Normandy, in his expedition against Philip, who had taken the opportunity of the troubles in England to invade that province. Those few Normans who bad survived their wounds, and had remained in the Isle of Ely, were all of our nation who went, the rest of his army being all composed of English. In a skirmish near the town of Mans my leg was broke and so shattered that it was forced to be cut off.

"I was now disabled from serving longer in the army; and accordingly, being discharged from the service, I retired to the place of my nativity, where, in extreme poverty, and frequent bad health from the many wounds I had received, I dragged on a miserable life to the age of sixty-three; my only pleasure being to recount the feats of my youth, in which narratives I generally exceeded the truth.

"It would be tedious and unpleasant to recount to you the several miseries I suffered after my return to Caen; let it suffice, they were so terrible that they induced Minos to compassionate me, and, notwithstanding the barbarities I had been guilty of in Northumberland, to suffer me to go once more back to earth."

CHAPTER XXII

What happened to Julian in the person of a tailor.

"Fortune now stationed me in a character which the ingratitude of mankind hath put them on ridiculing, though they owe to it not only a relief from the inclemencies of cold, to which they would otherwise be exposed, but likewise a considerable satisfaction of their vanity. The character I mean was that of a tailor; which, if we consider it with due attention, must be confessed to have in it great dignity and importance. For, in reality, who constitutes the different degrees between men but the tailor? the prince indeed gives the title, but it is the tailor who makes the man. To his labors are owing the respect of crowds, and the awe which great men inspire into their beholders, though these are too often unjustly attributed to other motives. Lastly, the admiration of the fair is most commonly to be placed to his account.

"I was just set up in my trade when I made three suits of fine clothes for king Stephen's coronation. I question whether the person who wears the rich coat hath so much pleasure and vanity in being admired in it, as we tailors have from that admiration; and perhaps a philosopher would say he is not so well entitled to it. I bustled on the day of the ceremony through the crowd, and it was with incredible delight I heard several say, as my clothes walked by, 'Bless me, was ever anything so fine as the earl of Devonshire? Sure he and Sir Hugh Bigot are the two best dressed men I ever saw.' Now both those suits were of my making.

"There would indeed be infinite pleasure in working for the courtiers, as they are generally genteel men, and show one's clothes to the best advantage, was it not for one small discouragement; this is, that they never pay. I solemnly protest, though I lost almost as much by the court in my life as I got by the city, I never carried a suit into the latter with half the satisfaction which I have done to the former; though from that I was certain of ready money, and from this almost as certain of no money at all.

"Courtiers may, however, be divided into two sorts, very essentially different from each other; into those who never intend to pay for their clothes; and those who do intend to pay for them, but never happen to be able. Of the latter sort are many of those young gentlemen whom we equip out for the army, and who are, unhappily for us, cut off before they arrive at preferment. This is the reason that tailors, in time of war, are mistaken for politicians by their inquisitiveness into the event of battles, one campaign very often proving the ruin of half-a-dozen of us. I am sure I had frequent reason to curse that fatal battle of Cardigan, where the Welsh defeated some of king Stephen's best troops, and where many a good suit of mine unpaid for, fell to the ground.

"The gentlemen of this honorable calling have fared much better in later ages than when I was of it; for now it seems the fashion is, when they apprehend their customer is not in the best circumstances, if they are not paid as soon as they carry home the suit, they charge him in their book as much again as it is worth, and then send a gentleman with a small scrip of parchment to demand the money. If this be not immediately paid the gentleman takes the beau with him to his house, where he locks him up till the tailor is contented: but in my time these scrips of parchment were not in use; and if the beau disliked paying for his clothes, as very often happened, we had no method of compelling him.

"In several of the characters which I have related to you, I apprehend I have sometimes forgot myself, and considered myself as really interested as I was when I personated them on earth. I have just now caught myself in the fact; for I have complained to you as bitterly of my customers as I formerly used to do when I was the tailor: but in reality, though there were some few persons of very great quality, and some others, who never paid their debts, yet those were but a few, and I had a method of repairing this loss. My customers I divided under three heads: those who paid ready money, those who paid slow, and those who never paid at all. The first of these I considered apart by themselves, as persons by whom I got a certain but small profit. The two last I lumped together, making those who paid slow contribute to repair my losses by those who did not pay at all. Thus, upon the whole, I was a very inconsiderable loser, and might have left a fortune to my family, had I not launched forth into expenses which swallowed up all my gains. I had a wife and two children. These indeed I kept frugally enough, for I half starved them; but I kept a mistress in a finer way, for whom I had a country-house, pleasantly situated on the Thames, elegantly fitted up and neatly furnished. This woman might very properly be called my mistress, for she was most absolutely so; and though her tenure was no higher than by my will, she domineered as tyrannically as if my chains had been riveted in the strongest manner. To all this I submitted, not through any adoration of her beauty, which was indeed but indifferent. Her charms consisted in little wantonnesses, which she knew admirably well to use in hours of dalliance, and which, I believe, are of all things the most delightful to a lover.

"She was so profusely extravagant, that it seemed as if she had an actual intent to ruin me. This I am sure of, if such had been her real intention, she could have taken no properer way to accomplish it; nay, I myself might appear to have had the same view: for, besides this extravagant mistress and my country-house, I kept likewise a brace of hunters, rather for that it was fashionable so to do than for any great delight I took in the sport, which I very little attended; not for want of leisure, for few noblemen had so much. All the work I ever did was taking measure, and that only of my greatest and best customers. I scare ever cut a piece of cloth in my life, nor was indeed much more able to fashion a coat than any gentleman in the kingdom. This made a skillful servant too necessary to me. He knew I must submit to any terms with, or any treatment from, him.

"He knew it was easier for him to find another such a tailor as me than for me to procure such another workman as him: for this reason he exerted the most notorious and cruel tyranny, seldom giving me a civil word; nor could the utmost condescension on my side, though attended with continual presents and rewards, and raising his wages, content or please him. In a word, he was as absolutely my master as was ever an ambitious, industrious prime minister over an indolent and voluptuous king. All my other journeymen paid more respect to him than to me; for they considered my favor as a necessary consequence of obtaining his.

"These were the most remarkable occurrences while I acted this part. Minos hesitated a few moments, and then bid me get back again, without assigning any reason."

CHAPTER XXIII

The life of alderman Julian.

"I now revisited England, and was born at London. My father was one of the magistrates of that city. He had eleven children, of whom I was the eldest. He had great success in trade, and grew extremely rich, but the largeness of his family rendered it impossible for him to leave me a fortune sufficient to live well on independent of business. I was accordingly brought up to be a fishmonger, in which capacity I myself afterwards acquired very considerable wealth.

"The same disposition of mind which in princes is called ambition is in subjects named faction. To this temper I was greatly addicted from my youth. I was, while a boy, a great partisan of prince John's against his brother Richard, during the latter's absence in the holy war and in his captivity. I was no more than one-and-twenty when I first began to make political speeches in public, and to endeavor to foment disquietude and discontent in the city. As I was pretty well qualified for this office, by a great fluency of words, an harmonious accent, a graceful delivery, and above all an invincible assurance, I had soon acquired some reputation among the younger citizens, and some of the weaker and more inconsiderate of a riper age. This, co-operating with my own natural vanity, made me extravagantly proud and supercilious. I soon began to esteem myself a man of some consequence, and to overlook persons every way my superiors.

"The famous Robin Hood, and his companion Little John, at this time made a considerable figure in Yorkshire. I took upon me to write a letter to the former, in the name of the city, inviting him to come to London, where I assured him of very good reception, signifying to him my own great weight and consequence, and how much I had disposed the citizens in his favor. Whether he received this letter or no I am not certain; but he never gave me any answer to it.

"A little afterwards one William Fitz-Osborn, or, as he was nicknamed, William Long-Beard, began to make a figure in the city. He was a bold and an impudent fellow, and had raised himself to great popularity with the rabble, by pretending to espouse their cause against the rich. I took this man's part, and made a public oration in his favor, setting him forth as a patriot, and one who had embarked in the cause of liberty: for which service he did not receive me with the acknowledgments I expected. However, as I thought I should easily gain the ascendant over this fellow, I continued still firm on his side, till the archbishop of Canterbury, with an armed force, put an end to his progress: for he was seized in Bowchurch, where he had taken refuge, and with nine of his accomplices hanged in chains.

"I escaped narrowly myself; for I was seized in the same church with the rest, and, as I had been very considerably engaged in the enterprise, the archbishop was inclined to make me an example; but my father's merit, who had advanced a considerable sum to queen Eleanor towards the king's ransom, preserved me.

"The consternation my danger had occasioned kept me some time quiet, and I applied myself very assiduously to my trade. I invented all manner of methods to enhance the price of fish, and made use of my utmost endeavors to engross as much of the business as possible in my own hands. By these means I acquired a substance which raised me to some little consequence in the city, but far from elevating me to that degree which I had formerly flattered myself with possessing at a time when I was totally insignificant; for, in a trading society, money must at least lay the foundation of all power and interest.

"But as it hath been remarked that the same ambition which sent Alexander into Asia brings the wrestler on the green; and as this same ambition is as incapable as quicksilver of lying still; so I, who was possessed perhaps of a share equal to what hath fired the blood of any of the heroes of antiquity, was no less restless and discontented with ease and quiet. My first endeavors were to make myself head of my company, which Richard I had just published, and soon afterwards I procured myself to be chosen alderman.

"Opposition is the only state which can give a subject an opportunity of exerting the disposition I was possessed of. Accordingly, king John was no sooner seated on his throne than I began to oppose his measures, whether right or wrong. It is true that monarch had faults enow. He was so abandoned to lust and luxury, that he addicted himself to the most extravagant excesses in both, while he indolently suffered the king of France to rob him of almost all his foreign dominions: my opposition therefore was justifiable enough, and if my motive from within had been as good as the occasion from without I should have had little to excuse; but, in truth, I sought nothing but my own preferment, by making myself formidable to the king, and then selling to him the interest of that party by whose means I had become so. Indeed, had the public good been my care, however zealously I might have opposed the beginning of his reign, I should not have scrupled to lend him my utmost assistance in this struggle between him and pope Innocent the third, in which he was so manifestly in the right; nor have suffered the insolence of that pope, and the power of the king of France, to have compelled him in the issue, basely to resign his crown into the hands of the former, and receive it again as a vassal; by means of which acknowledgment the pope afterwards claimed this kingdom as a tributary fief to be held of the papal chair; a claim which occasioned great uneasiness to many subsequent princes, and brought numberless calamities on the nation.

"As the king had, among other concessions, stipulated to pay an immediate sum of money to Pandulph, which he had great difficulty to raise, it was absolutely necessary for him to apply to the city, where my interest and popularity were so high that he had no hopes without my assistance. As I knew this, I took care to sell myself and country as high as possible. The terms I demanded, therefore, were a place, a pension, and a knighthood. All those were immediately consented to. I was forthwith knighted, and promised the other two.

"I now mounted the hustings, and, without any regard to decency or modesty, made as emphatical a speech in favor of the king as before I had done against him. In this speech I justified all those measures which I had before condemned, and pleaded as earnestly with my fellow-citizens to open their purses, as I had formerly done to prevail with them to keep them shut. But, alas! my rhetoric had not the effect I proposed. The consequence of my arguments was only contempt to myself. The people at first stared on one another, and afterwards began unanimously to express their dislike. An impudent fellow among them, reflecting on my trade, cried out, 'Stinking fish;' which was immediately reiterated through the whole crowd. I was then forced to slink away home; but I was not able to accomplish my retreat without being attended by the mob, who huzza'd me along the street with the repeated cries of 'Stinking fish.'

"I now proceeded to court, to inform his majesty of my faithful service, and how much I had suffered in his cause. I found by my first reception he had already heard of my success. Instead of thanking me for my speech, he said the city should repent of their obstinacy, for that he would show them who he was: and so saying, he immediately turned that part to me to which the toe of man hath so wonderful an affection, that it is very difficult, whenever it presents itself conveniently, to keep our toes from the most violent and ardent salutation of it.

"I was a little nettled at this behavior, and with some earnestness claimed the king's fulfilling his promise; but he retired without answering me. I then applied to some of the courtiers, who had lately professed great friendship to me, had eat at my house, and invited me to theirs: but not one would return me any answer, all running away from me as if I had been seized with some contagious distemper. I now found by experience, that as none can be so civil, so none can be ruder than a courtier.

"A few moments after the king's retiring I was left alone in the room to consider what I should do or whither I should turn myself. My reception in the city promised itself to be equal at least with what I found at court. However, there was my home, and thither it was necessary I should retreat for the present.

"But, indeed, bad as I apprehended my treatment in the city would be, it exceeded my expectation. I rode home on an ambling pad through crowds who expressed every kind of disregard and contempt; pelting me not only with the most abusive language, but with dirt. However, with much difficulty I arrived at last at my own house, with my bones whole, but covered over with filth.

"When I was got within my doors, and had shut them against the mob, who had pretty well vented their spleen, and seemed now contented to retire, my wife, whom I found crying over her children, and from whom I had hoped some comfort in my afflictions, fell upon me in the most outrageous manner. She asked me why I would venture on such a step, without consulting her; she said her advice might have been civilly asked, if I was resolved not to have been guided by it. That, whatever opinion I might have conceived of her understanding, the rest of the world thought better of it. That I had never failed when I had asked her counsel, nor ever succeeded without it; with much more of the same kind, too tedious to mention; concluding that it was a monstrous behavior to desert my party and come over to the court.

"An abuse which I took worse than all the rest, as she had been constantly for several years assiduous in railing at the opposition, in siding with the court-party, and begging me to come over to it; and especially after my mentioning the offer of knighthood to her, since which time she had continually interrupted my repose with dinning in my ears the folly of refusing honors and of adhering to a party and to principles by which I was certain of procuring no advantage to myself and my family.

"I had now entirely lost my trade, so that I had not the least temptation to stay longer in a city where I was certain of receiving daily affronts and rebukes. I therefore made up my affairs with the utmost expedition, and, scraping together all I could, retired into the country, where I spent the remainder of my days in universal contempt, being shunned by everybody, perpetually abused by my wife, and not much respected by my children

"Minos told me, though I had been a very vile fellow, he thought my sufferings made some atonement, and so bid me take the other trial."

CHAPTER XXIV

Julian recounts what happened to him while he was a poet.

"Rome was now the seat of my nativity, where I was born of a family more remarkable for honor than riches. I was intended for the church, and had a pretty good education; but my father dying while I was young, and leaving me nothing, for he had wasted his whole patrimony, I was forced to enter myself in the order of mendicants.

"When I was at school I had a knack of rhyming, which I unhappily mistook for genius, and indulged to my cost; for my verses drew on me only ridicule, and I was in contempt called the poet.

"This humor pursued me through my life. My first composition after I left school was a panegyric on pope Alexander IV, who then pretended a project of dethroning the king of Sicily. On this subject I composed a poem of about fifteen thousand lines, which with much difficulty I got to be presented to his holiness, of whom I expected great preferment as my reward; but I was cruelly disappointed: for when I had waited a year, without hearing any of the commendations I had flattered myself with receiving, and being now able to contain no longer, I applied to a Jesuit who was my relation, and had the pope's ear, to know what his holiness's opinion was of my work: he coldly answered me that he was at that time busied in concerns of too much importance to attend the reading of poems.

"However dissatisfied I might be, and really was, with this reception, and however angry I was with the pope? for whose understanding I entertained an immoderate contempt, I was not yet discouraged from a second attempt. Accordingly, I soon after produced another work, entitled, The Trojan Horse. This was an allegorical work, in which the church was introduced into the world in the same manner as that machine had been into Troy. The priests were the soldiers in its belly, and the heathen superstition the city to be destroyed by them. This poem was written in Latin. I remember some of the lines:

Mundanos scandit fatalis machina muros,
Farta sacerdotum turmis:exinde per alvum
Visi exire omnes, maguo cum murmure olentes.
Non aliter quam cum Ilumanis furibundus ab antris
It sonus et nares simul aura invadit hiantes.
Mille scatent et mille alii; trepidare timore
Ethnica gens coepit: falsi per inane volantes
Effugere Dei, Desertaque templa relinquunt.
Jam magnum crepitavit equus, mox orbis et alti
Ingemuere poli:tunc tu pater, ultimus omnium
Maxime Alexander, ventrem maturus equinum
Deseris, heu proles meliori digne parente."

"I believe Julian, had I not stopped him, would have gone through the whole poem (for, as I observed in most of the characters he related, the affections he had enjoyed while he personated them on earth still made some impression on him); but I begged him to omit the sequel of the poem, and proceed with his history. He then recollected himself, and, smiling at the observation which by intuition he perceived I had made, continued his narration as follows:

"I confess to you," says he, "that the delight in repeating our own works is so predominant in a poet, that I find nothing can totally root it out of the soul. Happy would it be for those persons if their hearers could be delighted in the same manner: but alas! hence that ingens solitudo complained of by Horace: for the vanity of mankind is so much greedier and more general than their avarice, that no beggar is so ill received by them as he who solicits their praise.

"This I sufficiently experienced in the character of a poet; for my company was shunned (I believe on this account chiefly) by my whole house: nay, there were few who would submit to hearing me read my poetry, even at the price of sharing in my provisions. The only person who gave me audience was a brother poet; he indeed fed me with commendation very liberally: but, as I was forced to hear and commend in my turn, I perhaps bought his attention dear enough.

"Well, sir, if my expectations of the reward I hoped from my first poem had balked me, I had now still greater reason to complain; for, instead of being preferred or commended for the second, I was enjoined a very severe penance by my superior, for ludicrously comparing the pope to a f--t. My poetry was now the jest of every company, except some few who spoke of it with detestation; and I found that, instead of recommending me to preferment, it had effectually barred me from all probability of attaining it.

"These discouragements had now induced me to lay down my pen and write no more. But, as Juvenal says,

Si discedas, Laqueo tenet ambitiosi
Consuetudo mali.

"I was an example of the truth of this assertion, for I soon betook myself again to my muse. Indeed, a poet hath the same happiness with a man who is dotingly fond of an ugly woman. The one enjoys his muse, and the other his mistress, with a pleasure very little abated by the esteem of the world, and only undervalues their taste for not corresponding with his own.

"It is unnecessary to mention any more of my poems; they had all the same fate; and though in reality some of my latter pieces deserved (I may now speak it without the imputation of vanity) a better success, as I had the character of a bad writer, I found it impossible ever to obtain the reputation of a good one. Had I possessed the merit of Homer I could have hoped for no applause; since it must have been a profound secret; for no one would now read a syllable of my writings.

"The poets of my age were, as I believe you know, not very famous. However, there was one of some credit at that time, though I have the consolation to know his works are all perished long ago. The malice, envy, and hatred I bore this man are inconceivable to any but an author, and an unsuccessful one; I never could bear to hear him well spoken of, and writ anonymous satires against him, though I had received obligations from him; indeed I believe it would have been an absolute impossibility for him at any rate to have made me sincerely his friend.

"I have heard an observation which was made by some one of later days, that there are no worse men than bad authors. A remark of the same kind hath been made on ugly women, and the truth of both stands on one and the same reason, viz., that they are both tainted with that cursed and detestable vice of envy; which, as it is the greatest torment to the mind it inhabits, so is it capable of introducing into it a total corruption, and of inspiring it to the commission of the most horrid crimes imaginable.

"My life was but short; for I soon pined myself to death with the vice I just now mentioned. Minos told me I was infinitely too bad for Elysium; and as for the other place, the devil had sworn he would never entertain a poet for Orpheus's sake: so I was forced to return again to the place from whence I came."

CHAPTER XXV

Julian performs the parts of a knight and a dancing-master.

"I now mounted the stage in Sicily, and became a knight-templar; but, as my adventures differ so little from those I have recounted you in the character of a common soldier, I shall not tire you with repetition. The soldier and the captain differ in reality so little from one another, that it requires an accurate judgment to distinguish them; the latter wears finer clothes, and in times of success lives somewhat more delicately; but as to everything else, they very nearly resemble one another.

"My next step was into France, where fortune assigned me the part of a dancing-master. I was so expert in my profession that I was brought to court in my youth, and had the heels of Philip de Valois, who afterwards succeeded Charles the Fair, committed to my direction.

"I do not remember that in any of the characters in which I appeared on earth I ever assumed to myself a greater dignity, or thought myself of more real importance, than now. I looked on dancing as the greatest excellence of human nature, and on myself as the greatest proficient in it. And, indeed, this seemed to be the general opinion of the whole court; for I was the chief instructor of the youth of both sexes, whose merit was almost entirely defined by the advances they made in that science which I had the honor to profess. As to myself, I was so fully persuaded of this truth, that I not only slighted and despised those who were ignorant of dancing, but I thought the highest character I could give any man was that he made a graceful bow: for want of which accomplishment I had a sovereign contempt for most persons of learning; nay, for some officers in the army, and a few even of the courtiers themselves.

"Though so little of my youth had been thrown away in what they call literature that I could hardly write and read, yet I composed a treatise on education; the first rudiments of which, as I taught, were to instruct a child in the science of coming handsomely into a room. In this I corrected many faults of my predecessors, particularly that of being too much in a hurry, and instituting a child in the sublimer parts of dancing before they are capable of making their honors.

"But as I have not now the same high opinion of my profession which I had then, I shall not entertain you with a long history of a life which consisted of borees and coupees. Let it suffice that I lived to a very old age and followed my business as long as I could crawl. At length I revisited my old friend Minos, who treated me with very little respect and bade me dance back again to earth.

"I did so, and was now once more born an Englishman, bred up to the church, and at length arrived to the station of a bishop.

"Nothing was so remarkable in this character as my always voting [10]."

BOOK II

CHAPTER VII

Wherein Anna Boleyn relates the history of her life.

"I am going now truly to recount a life which from the time of its ceasing has been, in the other world, the continual subject of the cavils of contending parties; the one making me as black as hell, the other as pure and innocent as the inhabitants of this blessed place; the mist of prejudice blinding their eyes, and zeal for what they themselves profess, making everything appear in that light which they think most conduces to its honor.

"My infancy was spent in my father's house, in those childish plays which are most suitable to that state, and I think this was one of the happiest parts of my life; for my parents were not among the number of those who look upon their children as so many objects of a tyrannic power, but I was regarded as the dear pledge of a virtuous love, and all my little pleasures were thought from their indulgence their greatest delight. At seven years old I was carried into France with the king's sister, who was married to the French king, where I lived with a person of quality, who was an acquaintance of my father's. I spent my time in learning those things necessary to give young persons of fashion a polite education, and did neither good nor evil, but day passed after day in the same easy way till I was fourteen; then began my anxiety, my vanity grew strong, and my heart fluttered with joy at every compliment paid to my beauty: and as the lady with whom I lived was of a gay, cheerful disposition, she kept a great deal of company, and my youth and charms made me the continual object of their admiration. I passed some little time in those exulting raptures which are felt by every woman perfectly satisfied with herself and with the behavior of others towards her: I was, when very young, promoted to be maid of honor to her majesty. The court was frequented by a young nobleman whose beauty was the chief subject of conversation in all assemblies of ladies. The delicacy of his person, added to a great softness in his manner, gave everything he said and did such an air of tenderness, that every woman he spoke to flattered herself with being the object of his love. I was one of those who was vain enough of my own charms to hope to make a conquest of him whom the whole court sighed for. I now thought every other object below my notice; yet the only pleasure I proposed to myself in this design was, the triumphing over that heart which I plainly saw all the ladies of the highest quality and the greatest beauty would have been proud of possessing. I was yet too young to be very artful; but nature, without any assistance, soon discovers to a man who is used to gallantry a woman's desire to be liked by him, whether that desire arises from any particular choice she makes of him, or only from vanity. He soon perceived my thoughts, and gratified my utmost wishes by constantly preferring me before all other women, and exerting his utmost gallantry and address to engage my affections. This sudden happiness, which I then thought the greatest I could have had, appeared visible in all my actions; I grew so gay and so full of vivacity that it made my person appear still to a better advantage, all my acquaintance pretending to be fonder of me than ever: though, young as I was, I plainly saw it was but pretense, for through all their endeavors to the contrary envy would often break forth in sly insinuations and malicious sneers, which gave me fresh matter of triumph, and frequent opportunities of insulting them, which I never let slip, for now first my female heart grew sensible of the spiteful pleasure of seeing another languish for what I enjoyed. Whilst I was in the height of my happiness her majesty fell ill of a languishing distemper, which obliged her to go into the country for the change of air: my place made it necessary for me to attend her, and which way he brought it about I can't imagine, but my young hero found means to be one of that small train that waited on my royal mistress, although she went as privately as possible. Hitherto all the interviews I had ever had with him were in public, and I only looked on him as the fitter object to feed that pride which had no other view but to show its power; but now the scene was quite changed. My rivals, were all at a distance: the place we went to was as charming as the most agreeable natural situation, assisted by the greatest art, could make it; the pleasant solitary walks the singing of birds, the thousand pretty romantic scenes this delightful place afforded, gave a sudden turn to my mind; my whole soul was melted into softness, and all my vanity was fled. My spark was too much used to affairs of this nature not to perceive this change; at first the profuse transports of his joy made me believe him wholly mine, and this belief gave me such happiness that no language affords words to express it, and can be only known to those who have felt it. But this was of a very short duration, for I soon found I had to do with one of those men whose only end in the pursuit of a woman is to make her fall a victim to an insatiable desire to be admired. His designs had succeeded, and now he every day grew colder, and, as if by infatuation, my passion every day increased; and, notwithstanding all my resolutions and endeavors to the contrary, my rage at the disappointment at once both of my love and pride, and at the finding a passion fixed in my breast I knew not how to conquer, broke out into that inconsistent behavior which must always be the consequence of violent passions. One moment I reproached him, the next I grew to tenderness and blamed myself, and thought I fancied what was not true: he saw my struggle and triumphed in it; but, as he had not witnesses enough there of his victory to give him the full enjoyment of it, he grew weary of the country and returned to Paris, and left me in a condition it is utterly impossible to describe. My mind was like a city up in arms, all confusion; and every new thought was a fresh disturber of my peace. Sleep quite forsook me, and the anxiety I suffered threw me into a fever which had like to have cost me my life. With great care I recovered, but the violence of the distemper left such a weakness on my body that the disturbance of my mind was greatly assuaged; and now I began to comfort myself in the reflection that this gentleman's being a finished coquette was very likely the only thing could have preserved me; for he was the only man from whom I was ever in any danger. By that time I was got tolerably well we returned to Paris; and I confess I both wished and feared to see this cause of all my pain: however, I hoped, by the help of my resentment, to be able to meet him with indifference. This employed my thoughts till our arrival. The next day there was a very full court to congratulate the queen on her recovery; and amongst the rest my love appeared dressed and adorned as if he designed some new conquest. Instead of seeing a woman he despised and slighted, he approached me with that assured air which is common to successful coxcombs. At the same time I perceived I was surrounded by all those ladies who were on his account my greatest enemies, and, in revenge, wished for nothing more than to see me make a ridiculous figure. This situation so perplexed my thoughts, that when he came near enough to speak to me, I fainted away in his arms. Had I studied which way I could gratify him most, it was impossible to have done anything to have pleased him more. Some that stood by brought smelling-bottles, and used means for my recovery; and I was welcomed to returning life by all those repartees which women enraged by envy are capable of venting. One cried 'Well, I never thought my lord had anything so frightful in his person or so fierce in his manner as to strike a young lady dead at the sight of him.' 'No, no,' says another, 'some ladies' senses are more apt to be hurried by agreeable than disagreeable objects.' With many more such sort of speeches which showed more malice than wit. This not being able to bear, trembling, and with but just strength enough to move, I crawled to my coach and hurried home. When I was alone, and thought on what had happened to me in a public court, I was at first driven to the utmost despair; but afterwards, when I came to reflect, I believe this accident contributed more to my being cured of my passion than any other could have done. I began to think the only method to pique the man who had used me so barbarously, and to be revenged on my spiteful rivals, was to recover that beauty which was then languid and had lost its luster, to let them see I had still charms enough to engage as many lovers as I could desire, and that I could yet rival them who had thus cruelly insulted me. These pleasing hopes revived my sinking spirits, and worked a more effectual cure on me than all the philosophy and advice of the wisest men could have done. I now employed all my time and care in adorning my person, and studying the surest means of engaging the affections of others, while I myself continued quite indifferent; for I resolved for the future, if ever one soft thought made its way to my heart, to fly the object of it, and by new lovers to drive the image from my breast. I consulted my glass every morning, and got such a command of my countenance that I could suit it to the different tastes of variety of lovers; and though I was young, for I was not yet above seventeen, yet my public way of life gave me such continual opportunities of conversing with men, and the strong desire I now had of pleasing them led me to make such constant observations on everything they said or did, that I soon found out the different methods of dealing with them. I observed that most men generally liked in women what was most opposite to their own characters; therefore to the grave solid man of sense I endeavored to appear sprightly and full of spirit; to the witty and gay, soft and languishing; to the amorous (for they want no increase of their passions), cold and reserved; to the fearful and backward, warm and full of fire; and so of all the rest. As to beaux, and all of those sort of men, whose desires are centered in the satisfaction of their vanity, I had learned by sad experience the only way to deal with them was to laugh at them and let their own good opinion of themselves be the only support of their hopes. I knew, while I could get other followers, I was sure of them; for the only sign of modesty they ever give is that of not depending on their own judgments, but following the opinions of the greatest number. Thus furnished with maxims, and grown wise by past errors, I in a manner began the world again: I appeared in all public places handsomer and more lively than ever, to the amazement of every one who saw me and had heard of the affair between me and my lord. He himself was much surprised and vexed at this sudden change, nor could he account how it was possible for me so soon to shake off those chains he thought he had fixed on me for life; nor was he willing to lose his conquest in this manner. He endeavored by all means possible to talk to me again of love, but I stood fixed to my resolution (in which I was greatly assisted by the crowd of admirers that daily surrounded me) never to let him explain himself: for, notwithstanding all my pride, I found the first impression the heart receives of love is so strong that it requires the most vigilant care to prevent a relapse. Now I lived three years in a constant round of diversions, and was made the perfect idol of all the men that came to court of all ages and all characters. I had several good matches offered me, but I thought none of them equal to my merit; and one of my greatest pleasures was to see those women who had pretended to rival me often glad to marry those whom I had refused. Yet, notwithstanding this great success of my schemes, I cannot say I was perfectly happy; for every woman that was taken the least notice of, and every man that was insensible to my arts, gave me as much pain as all the rest gave me pleasure; and sometimes little underhand plots which were laid against my designs would succeed in spite of my care: so that I really began to grow weary of this manner of life, when my father, returning from his embassy in France, took me home with him, and carried me to a little pleasant country-house, where there was nothing grand or superfluous, but everything neat and agreeable. There I led a life perfectly solitary. At first the time hung very heavy on my hands, and I wanted all kind of employment, and I had very like to have fallen into the height of the vapors, from no other reason but from want of knowing what to do with myself. But when I had lived here a little time I found such a calmness in my mind, and such a difference between this and the restless anxieties I had experienced in a court, that I began to share the tranquillity that visibly appeared in everything round me. I set myself to do works of fancy, and to raise little flower-gardens, with many such innocent rural amusements; which, although they are not capable of affording any great pleasure, yet they give that serene turn to the mind which I think much preferable to anything else human nature is made susceptible of. I now resolved to spend the rest of my days here, and that nothing should allure me from that sweet retirement, to be again tossed about with tempestuous passions of any kind. Whilst I was in this situation, my lord Percy, the earl of Northumberland's eldest son, by an accident of losing his way after a fox-chase, was met by my father, about a mile from our house; he came home with him, only with a design of dining with us, but was so taken with me that he stayed three days. I had too much experience in all affairs of this kind not to see presently the influence I had on him; but I was at that time so entirely free from all ambition, that even the prospect of being a countess had no effect on me; and I then thought nothing in the world could have bribed me to have changed my way of life. This young lord, who was just in his bloom, found his passion so strong, he could not endure a long absence, but returned again in a week, and endeavored, by all the means he could think of, to engage me to return his affection. He addressed me with that tenderness and respect which women on earth think can flow from nothing but real love; and very often told me that, unless he could be so happy as by his assiduity and care to make himself agreeable to me, although he knew my father would eagerly embrace any proposal from him, yet he would suffer that last of miseries of never seeing me more rather than owe his own happiness to anything that might be the least contradiction to my inclinations. This manner of proceeding had something in it so noble and generous, that by degrees it raised a sensation in me which I know not how to describe, nor by what name to call it: it was nothing like my former passion: for there was no turbulence, no uneasy waking nights attending it, but all I could with honor grant to oblige him appeared to me to be justly due to his truth and love, and more the effect of gratitude than of any desire of my own. The character I had heard of him from my father at my first returning to England, in discoursing of the young nobility, convinced me that if I was his wife I should have the perpetual satisfaction of knowing every action of his must be approved by all the sensible part of mankind; so that very soon I began to have no scruple left but that of leaving my little scene of quietness, and venturing again into the world. But this, by his continual application and submissive behavior, by degrees entirely vanished, and I agreed he should take his own time to break it to my father, whose consent he was not long in obtaining; for such a match was by no means to be refused. There remained nothing now to be done but to prevail with the earl of Northumberland to comply with what his son so ardently desired; for which purpose he set out immediately for London, and begged it as the greatest favor that I would accompany my father, who was also to go thither the week following. I could not refuse his request, and as soon as we arrived in town he flew to me with the greatest raptures to inform me his father was so good that, finding his happiness depended on his answer, he had given him free leave to act in this affair as would best please himself, and that he had now no obstacle to prevent his wishes. It was then the beginning of the winter, and the time for our marriage was fixed for the latter end of March: the consent of all parties made his access to me very easy, and we conversed together both with innocence and pleasure. As his fondness was so great that he contrived all the methods possible to keep me continually in his sight, he told me one morning he was commanded by his father to attend him to court that evening, and begged I would be so good as to meet him there. I was now so used to act as he would have me that I made no difficulty of complying with his desire. Two days after this, I was very much surprised at perceiving such a melancholy in his countenance, and alteration in his behavior, as I could no way account for; but, by importunity, at last I got from him that cardinal Wolsey, for what reason he knew not, had peremptorily forbid him to think any more of me: and, when he urged that his father was not displeased with it, the cardinal, in his imperious manner, answered him, he should give his father such convincing reasons why it would be attended with great inconveniences, that he was sure he could bring him to be of his opinion. On which he turned from him, and gave him no opportunity of replying. I could not imagine what design the cardinal could have in intermeddling in this match, and I was still more perplexed to find that my father treated my lord Percy with much more coldness than usual; he too saw it, and we both wondered what could possibly be the cause of all this. But it was not long before the mystery was all made clear by my father, who, sending for me one day into his chamber, let me into a secret which was as little wished for as expected. He began with the surprising effects of youth and beauty, and the madness of letting go those advantages they might procure us till it was too late, when we might wish in vain to bring them back again. I stood amazed at this beginning; he saw my confusion, and bid me sit down and attend to what he was going to tell me, which was of the greatest consequence; and he hoped I would be wise enough to take his advice, and act as he should think best for my future welfare. He then asked me if I should not be much pleased to be a queen? I answered, with the greatest earnestness, that, so far from it, I would not live in a court again to be the greatest queen in the world; that I had a lover who was both desirous and able to raise my station even beyond my wishes. I found this discourse was very displeasing; my father frowned, and called me a romantic fool, and said if I would hearken to him he could make me a queen; for the cardinal had told him that the king, from the time he saw me at court the other night, liked me, and intended to get a divorce from his wife, and to put me in her place; and ordered him to find some method to make me a maid of honor to her present majesty, that in the meantime he might have an opportunity of seeing me. It is impossible to express the astonishment these words threw me into; and, notwithstanding that the moment before, when it appeared at so great a distance, I was very sincere in my declaration how much it was against my will to be raised so high, yet now the prospect came nearer, I confess my heart fluttered, and my eyes were dazzled with a view of being seated on a throne.

"My imagination presented before me all the pomp, power and greatness that attend a crown; and I was so perplexed I knew not what to answer, but remained as silent as if I had lost the use of my speech. My father, who guessed what it was that made me in this condition, proceeded to bring all the arguments he thought most likely to bend me to his will; at last I recovered from this dream of grandeur, and begged him, by all the most endearing names I could think of, not to urge me dishonorably to forsake the man who I was convinced would raise me to an empire if in his power, and who had enough in his power to give me all I desired. But he was deaf to all I could say, and insisted that by next week I should prepare myself to go to court: he bid me consider of it, and not prefer a ridiculous notion of honor to the real interest of my whole family; but, above all things, not to disclose what he had trusted me with. On which he left me to my own thoughts. When I was alone I reflected how little real tenderness this behavior showed to me, whose happiness he did not at all consult, but only looked on me as a ladder, on which he could climb to the height of his own ambitious desires: and when I thought on his fondness for me in my infancy I could impute it to nothing but either the liking me as a plaything or the gratification of his vanity in my beauty. But I was too much divided between a crown and my engagement to lord Percy to spend much time in thinking of anything else; and, although my father had positively forbid me, yet, when he came next, I could not help acquainting him with all that had passed, with the reserve only of the struggle in my own mind on the first mention of being a queen. I expected he would have received the news with the greatest agonies; but he showed no vast emotion: however, he could not help turning pale, and, taking me by the hand, looked at me with an air of tenderness, and said, 'If being a queen would make you happy, and it is in your power to be so, I would not for the world prevent it, let me suffer what I will.' This amazing greatness of mind had on me quite the contrary effect from what it ought to have had; for, instead of increasing my love for him it almost put an end to it, and I began to think, if he could part with me, the matter was not much. And I am convinced, when any man gives up the possession of a woman whose consent he has once obtained, let his motive be ever so generous, he will disoblige her. I could not help showing my dissatisfaction, and told him I was very glad this affair sat so easily on him. He had not power to answer, but was so suddenly struck with this unexpected ill-natured turn I gave his behavior, that he stood amazed for some time, and then bowed and left me. Now I was again left to my own reflections; but to make anything intelligible out of them is quite impossible: I wished to be a queen, and wished I might not be one: I would have my lord Percy happy without me; and yet I would not have the power of my charms be so weak that he could bear the thought of life after being disappointed in my love. But the result of all these confused thoughts was a resolution to obey my father. I am afraid there was not much duty in the case, though at that time I was glad to take hold of that small shadow to save me from looking on my own actions in the true light. When my lover came again I looked on him with that coldness that he could not bear, on purpose to rid myself of all importunity: for since I had resolved to use him ill I regarded him as the monument of my shame, and his every look appeared to me to upbraid me. My father soon carried me to court; there I had no very hard part to act; for, with the experience I had had of mankind, I could find no great difficulty in managing a man who liked me, and for whom I not only did not care but had an utter aversion to: but this aversion he believed to be virtue; for how credulous is a man who has an inclination to believe! And I took care sometimes to drop words of cottages and love, and how happy the woman was who fixed her affections on a man in such a station of life that she might show her love without being suspected of hypocrisy or mercenary views. All this was swallowed very easily by the amorous king, who pushed on the divorce with the utmost impetuosity, although the affair lasted a good while, and I remained most part of the time behind the curtain. Whenever the king mentioned it to me I used such arguments against it as I thought the most likely to make him the more eager for it; begging that, unless his conscience was really touched, he would not on my account give any grief to his virtuous queen; for in being her handmaid I thought myself highly honored; and that I would not only forego a crown, but even give up the pleasure of ever seeing him more, rather than wrong my royal mistress. This way of talking, joined to his eager desire to possess my person, convinced the king so strongly of my exalted merit, that he thought it a meritorious act to displace the woman (whom he could not have so good an opinion of, because he was tired of her), and to put me in her place. After about a year's stay at court, as the king's love to me began to be talked of, it was thought proper to remove me, that there might be no umbrage given to the queen's party. I was forced to comply with this, though greatly against my will; for I was very jealous that absence might change the king's mind. I retired again with my father to his country-seat, but it had no longer those charms for me which I once enjoyed there; for my mind was now too much taken up with ambition to make room for any other thoughts. During my stay here, my royal lover often sent gentlemen to me with messages and letters, which I always answered in the manner I thought would best bring about my designs, which were to come back again to court. In all the letters that passed between us there was something so kingly and commanding in his, and so deceitful and submissive in mine, that I sometimes could not help reflecting on the difference betwixt this correspondence and that with lord Percy; yet I was so pressed forward by the desire of a crown, I could not think of turning back. In all I wrote I continually praised his resolution of letting me be at a distance from him, since at this time it conduced indeed to my honor; but, what was of ten times more weight with me, I thought it was necessary for his; and I would sooner suffer anything in the world than be any means of hurt to him, either in his interest or reputation. I always gave some hints of ill health, with some reflections how necessary the peace of the mind was to that of the body. By these means I brought him to recall me again by the most absolute command, which I, for a little time, artfully delayed (for I knew the impatience of his temper would not bear any contradictions), till he made my father in a manner force me to what I most wished, with the utmost appearance of reluctance on my side. When I had gained this point I began to think which way I could separate the king from the queen; for hitherto they lived in the same house. The lady Mary, the queen's daughter, being then about sixteen, I sought for emissaries of her own age that I could confide in, to instill into her mind disrespectful thoughts of her father, and make a jest of the tenderness of his conscience about the divorce. I knew she had naturally strong passions, and that young people of that age are apt to think those that pretend to be their friends are really so, and only speak their minds freely. I afterwards contrived to have every word she spoke of him carried to the king, who took it all as I could wish, and fancied those things did not come at first from the young lady, but from her mother. He would often talk of it to me, and I agreed with him in his sentiments; but then, as a great proof of my goodness, I always endeavored to excuse her, by saying a lady so long time used to be a royal queen might naturally be a little exasperated with those she fancied would throw her from that station she so justly deserved. By these sort of plots I found the way to make the king angry with the queen; for nothing is easier than to make a man angry with a woman he wants to be rid of, and who stands in the way between him and his pleasure; so that now the king, on the pretense of the queen's obstinacy in a point where his conscience was so tenderly concerned, parted with her. Everything was now plain before me; I had nothing farther to do but to let the king alone to his own desires; and I had no reason to fear, since they had carried him so far, but that they would urge him on to do everything I aimed at. I was created marchioness of Pembroke. This dignity sat very easy on me; for the thoughts of a much higher title took from me all feeling of this; and I looked upon being a marchioness as a trifle, not that I saw the bauble in its true light, but because it fell short of what I had figured to myself I should soon obtain. The king's desires grew very impatient, and it was not long before I was privately married to him. I was no sooner his wife than I found all the queen come upon me; I felt myself conscious of royalty, and even the faces of my most intimate acquaintance seemed to me to be quite strange. I hardly knew them: height had turned my head, and I was like a man placed on a monument, to whose sight all creatures at a great distance below him appear like so many little pigmies crawling about on the earth; and the prospect so greatly delighted me, that I did not presently consider that in both cases descending a few steps erected by human hands would place us in the number of those very pigmies who appeared so despicable. Our marriage was kept private for some time, for it was not thought proper to make it public (the affair of the divorce not being finished) till the birth of my daughter Elizabeth made it necessary. But all who saw me knew it; for my manner of speaking and acting was so much changed with my station, that all around me plainly perceived I was sure I was a queen. While it was a secret I had yet something to wish for; I could not be perfectly satisfied till all the world was acquainted with my fortune: but when my coronation was over, and I was raised to the height of my ambition, instead of finding myself happy, I was in reality more miserable than ever; for, besides that the aversion I had naturally to the king was much more difficult to dissemble after marriage than before, and grew into a perfect detestation, my imagination, which had thus warmly pursued a crown, grew cool when I was in the possession of it, and gave me time to reflect what mighty matter I had gained by all this bustle; and I often used to think myself in the case of the fox-hunter, who, when he has toiled and sweated all day in the chase as if some unheard-of blessing was to crown his success, finds at last all he has got by his labor is a stinking nauseous animal. But my condition was yet worse than his; for he leaves the loathsome wretch to be torn by his hounds, whilst I was obliged to fondle mine, and meanly pretend him to be the object of my love. For the whole time I was in this envied, this exalted state, I led a continual life of hypocrisy, which I now know nothing on earth can compensate. I had no companion but the man I hated. I dared not disclose my sentiments to any person about me, nor did any one presume to enter into any freedom of conversation with me; but all who spoke to me talked to the queen, and not to me; for they would have said just the same things to a dressed-up puppet, if the king had taken a fancy to call it his wife. And as I knew every woman in the court was my enemy, from thinking she had much more right than I had to the place I filled, I thought myself as unhappy as if I had been placed in a wild wood, where there was no human creature for me to speak to, in a continual fear of leaving any traces of my footsteps, lest I should be found by some dreadful monster, or stung by snakes and adders; for such are spiteful women to the objects of their envy. In this worst of all situations I was obliged to hide my melancholy and appear cheerful. This threw me into an error the other way, and I sometimes fell into a levity in my behavior that was afterwards made use of to my disadvantage. I had a son deadborn, which I perceived abated something of the king's ardor; for his temper could not brook the least disappointment. This gave me no uneasiness; for, not considering the consequences, I could not help being best pleased when I had least of his company. Afterwards I found he had cast his eyes on one of my maids of honor; and, whether it was owing to any art of hers, or only to the king's violent passions, I was in the end used even worse than my former mistress had been by my means. The decay of the king's affection was presently seen by all those court-sycophants who continually watch the motions of royal eyes; and the moment they found they could be heard against me they turned my most innocent actions and words, nay, even my very looks, into proofs of the blackest crimes. The king, who was impatient to enjoy his new love, lent a willing ear to all my accusers, who found ways of making him jealous that I was false to his bed. He would not so easily have believed anything against me before, but he was now glad to flatter himself that he had found a reason to do just what he had resolved upon without a reason; and on some slight pretenses and hearsay evidence I was sent to the Tower, where the lady who was my greatest enemy was appointed to watch me and lie in the same chamber with me. This was really as bad a punishment as my death, for she insulted me with those keen reproaches and spiteful witticisms, which threw me into such vapors and violent fits that I knew not what I uttered in this condition. She pretended I had confessed talking ridiculous stuff with a set of low fellows whom I had hardly ever taken notice of, as could have imposed on none but such as were resolved to believe. I was brought to my trial, and, to blacken me the more, accused of conversing criminally with my own brother, whom indeed I loved extremely well, but never looked on him in any other light than as my friend. However, I was condemned to be beheaded, or burnt, as the king pleased; and he was graciously pleased, from the great remains of his love, to choose the mildest sentence. I was much less shocked at this manner of ending my life than I should have been in any other station: but I had had so little enjoyment from the time I had been a queen, that death was the less dreadful to me. The chief things that lay on my conscience were the arts I made use of to induce the king to part with the queen, my ill usage of lady Mary, and my jilting lord Percy. However, I endeavored to calm my mind as well as I could, and hoped these crimes would be forgiven me; for in other respects

I had led a very innocent life, and always did all the good-natured actions I found any opportunity of doing. From the time I had it in my power, I gave a great deal of money amongst the poor; I prayed very devoutly, and went to my execution very composedly. Thus I lost my life at the age of twenty-nine, in which short time I believe I went through more variety of scenes than many people who live to be very old. I had lived in a court, where I spent my time in coquetry and gayety; I had experienced what it was to have one of those violent passions which makes the mind all turbulence and anxiety; I had had a lover whom I esteemed and valued, and at the latter part of my life I was raised to a station as high as the vainest woman could wish. But in all these various changes I never enjoyed any real satisfaction, unless in the little time I lived retired in the country free from all noise and hurry, and while I was conscious I was the object of the love and esteem of a man of sense and honor."

On the conclusion of this history Minos paused for a small time, and then ordered the gate to be thrown open for Anna Boleyn's admittance on the consideration that whoever had suffered being the queen for four years, and been sensible during all that time of the real misery which attends that exalted station, ought to be forgiven whatever she had done to obtain it. [11]

Footnotes:

[Footnote 1: Some doubt whether this should not be rather 1641, which is a date more agreeable to the account given of it in the introduction: but then there are some passages which seem to relate to transactions infinitely later, even within this year or two. To say the truth there are difficulties attending either conjecture; so the reader may take which he pleases.]

[Footnote 2: Eyes are not perhaps so properly adapted to a spiritual substance; but we are here, as in many other places, obliged to use corporeal terms to make ourselves the better understood.]

[Footnote 3: This is the dress in which the god appears to mortals at the theaters. One of the offices attributed to this god by the ancients, was to collect the ghosts as a shepherd doth a flock of sheep, and drive them with his wand into the other world.]

[Footnote 4: Those who have read of the gods sleeping in Homer will not be surprised at this happening to spirits.]

[Footnote 5: A particular lady of quality is meant here; but every lady of quality, or no quality, are welcome to apply the character to themselves.]

[Footnote 6: We have before made an apology for this language, which we here repeat for the last time; though the heart may, we hope, be metaphorically used here with more propriety than when we apply those passions to the body which belong to the soul.]

[Footnote 7: That we may mention it once for all, in the panegyrical part of this work some particular person is always meant: but, in the satirical, nobody.]

[Footnote 8: These ladies, I believe, by their names, presided over the leprosy, king's-evil, and scurvy.]

[Footnote 9: This silly story is told as a solemn truth (i.e., that St. James really appeared in the manner this fellow is described) by Mariana, 1.7, Section 78.]

[Footnote 10: Here part of the manuscript is lost, and that a very considerable one, as appears by the number of the next book and chapter, which contains, I find, the history of Anna Boleyn; but as to the manner in which it was introduced, or to whom the narrative is told, we are totally left in the dark. I have only to remark, that this chapter is, in the original, writ in a woman's hand: and, though the observations in it are, I think, as excellent as any in the whole volume, there seems to be a difference in style between this and the preceding chapters; and, as it is the character of a woman which is related, I am inclined to fancy it was really written by one of that sex.]

[Footnote 11: Here ends this curious manuscript; the rest being destroyed in rolling up pens, tobacco, &c. It is to be hoped heedless people will henceforth be more cautious what they burn, or use to other vile purposes; especially when they consider the fate which had likely to have befallen the divine Milton, and that the works of Homer were probably discovered in some chandlers shop in Greece.]

www.ingramcontent.com/pod-product-compliance
Lightning Source LLC
Chambersburg PA
CBHW061456170626
46811CB00004B/1533